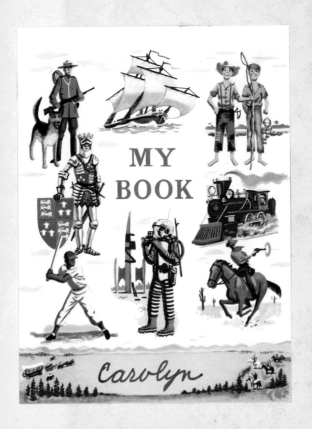

MY
BOOK

Carolyn

Junior Miss

Junior Miss

BY SALLY BENSON

THE SUN DIAL PRESS

Garden City, New York

1942
THE SUN DIAL PRESS

This book is for
BARBARA BENSON

Contents

1. Junior Miss   9

2. A Furtive Tear   27

3. Daddy Dear   45

4. Madame la Marquise, Toujours Exquise   61

5. For Posterity   75

6. The Paragon   91

7. The Best Things Come in Small Packages 107

8. New Leaf   125

9. Bury Me Not   147

10. Appreciation of Art   159

11. Les Temps Perdus   177

12. Primrose Path   195

1

Junior Miss

ONE

Junior Miss

THE coat was advertised in Sunday's paper. There was a picture of it which showed a lovely squirrel collar and a belt that tied in a soft bow. Mrs. Graves saw it and called to Judy, who was reading the funny paper. "Isn't this nice-looking?" she asked.

Judy couldn't believe her eyes. At first she thought that her mother must be thinking of getting the coat for Lois, but reason told her that Lois had a winter coat, new last year, and that her own coat was too tight across the shoulders and too short in the sleeves. She drew in her breath so sharply and with such rapture that she hiccoughed. Mrs. Graves frowned. "Judy!" she said, mechanically.

"Fur!" Judy gasped. "Oh, boy!"

She leaned over her mother's shoulder to read the advertisement. "Coat of feathery wool tweed, gossamer soft, with lamb's-wool interlining, dashing squirrel collar which buttons snugly under the chin, and fitted waist to give you the new Continental look. Comes in colors as gay as the autumn woods. Brown, grape, leaf red, and henna. Sizes 7 to 14. Price—$29.50."

"Well, my dear, do you like it?" Mrs. Graves asked.

"Like it!" Judy repeated. "It's perfect. Oh, Mother!"

"Let's see it," Lois said. She folded her part of the funny paper and laid it neatly on the table. When she walked, she took short, prim steps and her skirt swung from side to side from her slender, childish hips. She looked at the coat critically.

"It's *awfully* nice," she agreed, "except that the belt is going to look peculiar, to say the least."

Her eyes travelled coldly to Judy's middle. "Judy shouldn't wear a belt, especially a belt

12

with a *bow*. She'll be excruciating in it. It will make her look like a sack of meal."

"I suppose you're right," Mrs. Graves said.

"She's not!" Judy cried. "She's jealous, that's all. She doesn't want me to have a coat with a fur collar because *she* has a coat with a fur collar, and she wants to be the *only* one."

Lois laughed tolerantly. "Don't be absurd," she said. "*Get* the coat, by all means, if you don't mind looking like a sack of meal. Or worse."

"What do you mean *worse*?" Judy asked grimly.

"You know," Lois said meaningly. "What I told you."

Judy's face was white and her lips trembled. "I won't."

"Oh, yes you will. With that big bow."

"Will what?" Mrs. Graves asked. "What are you two talking about?"

"She's mean," Judy said. "She wants to spoil everything, and I won't let her."

"Will what?" Mrs. Graves repeated.

13

"Look pregnant." Judy blurted it out.

Mrs. Graves put the paper down in her lap. "I have never," she told them sternly, "heard such dreadful talk. You ought to be ashamed of yourselves."

"Lois was the one. She's always saying it."

"Go to your room, Lois, and stay there until I say you may come out," Mrs. Graves said. Her eyes followed Lois's slim figure as she left, and she sighed. "Well, we'll see."

"Please," Judy begged. She stood in front of her mother, her dark-brown eyebrows meeting in a line as she frowned anxiously.

Mrs. Graves leaned forward and pulled at her daughter's skirt. "I don't know why your skirts always hike up that way. It must be the way you sit on them."

Judy smoothed her dress over her round, firm little stomach. "Please," she said.

"I'll see."

"Can we go tomorrow?" she asked.

"If we go at all, we'll go next Saturday morning," Mrs. Graves answered. "And I don't want to hear another word about it."

14

"But it might be gone by next Saturday." Judy had a sharp vision of dozens of little girls snatching at the coats and wearing them out of the store, looking triumphantly Continental.

"Don't be silly," Mrs. Graves said. "They have hundreds of them."

Judy walked slowly back to her chair and picked up the funny paper, but it had lost its flavor. She went quietly to her mother's room and stood in front of the long mirror that was set in the door of the closet. She was tall for her twelve years and heavily built. From her shoulders to her knees she was entirely shapeless, which gave her a square, broad look in spite of her height. Her summer tan had faded and her face had a rather ghastly yellow tinge. Below her skirt, which was too short for her, her legs were hard, muscular, and covered with scratches. Her dress, a soft-blue one, smocked at the sleeves, was supposed to hang gracefully from the shoulders in straight folds, but instead it pulled as though she had been stuffed into it. She wore two rings on her fingers—an aquamarine and a turquoise in gold settings. She had

15

outgrown them and they drew her fingers in at their bases and made them look like sausages. She wore two charm bracelets of a brassy color and a locket and chain that fastened so tightly around her neck it seemed it might throttle her. In the locket was a rather dim snapshot of a kitten and a clear picture of Tyrone Power, clipped from a movie magazine. Her dark-brown hair hung straight below her ears and was held in place by numerous bobbie pins and two ready-made bows. Her toenails, under her wool socks and scuffed brown oxfords, were painted with a decadent pink mother-of-pearl polish.

She sucked in her stomach, held her breath, and pulled her dress in at the waist. And, while the change in her silhouette reflected in the mirror was almost imperceptible, her eyes shone with a terrible optimism.

She lived through the week that followed slightly breathless from holding her stomach in and quite faint from going without her lunch. She wore her old coat tolerantly to school each

day and treated it with disrespect, throwing it
on the floor of the coatroom and kicking it into
the closet of her room at night. And at recess,
in the warm security of friendship, she boasted
a little. "Oh, bilge!" she exclaimed. "I just now
remembered that I've got to go *shopping* Saturday. Have to get a new coat and stuff."

Her best friend murmured, "How too filthy,"
with understanding.

"Oh, foul," Judy said complacently. "Of,
course, *this* poor old thing's a wreck. I always
loathed it, anyway. I wouldn't have picked it
out in the first place if it hadn't been for snotty
old Lois. *She's* always right, of course."

"Oh, needless to say."

"But," Judy went on, "as long as what will be
will be, I might as well get something stunning
while I'm about it. Something with a fur collar
and fitted."

"If charming Lois doesn't butt in."

"Oh, I guess charming Lois won't butt in *this*
time. I think fur softens the face, don't you?"

"Definitely."

When she awoke Saturday morning, she
had the half-sick feeling of anticipation of
Christmas Eve. She bathed and dressed carefully, rubbing a little talcum powder on her
nose and looking at her face closely to make
sure it didn't show. She was on time for breakfast.

"Good morning, Judy," her mother said.
"You have a little talcum powder on your nose,
dear. Rub it off."

Across the table, Lois smiled and her eyes
closed like a cat's.

"Well, Judy," her father said, "I hear you're
going shopping today."

She sighed. "I suppose so."

"You *suppose* so," Lois jeered. "She hasn't
been able to eat for a week."

"Mother," Judy pleaded, "does *she* have to
come with us?"

"She does," Mrs. Graves answered. "Now,
not so early in the morning, girls, please!"

As Judy helped herself to two tablespoons of
sugar, Lois shook her head meaningly. "Better

watch yourself," she said. "Not that it isn't too late, P. K."

P. K. meant Powerful Katrinka.

"You're getting too old to tease your sister every minute, Lois," Mrs. Graves said.

"Fifteen isn't so old," Judy scoffed. "She tells everyone she's sixteen. Fifteen is just a baby age, really."

"If I'm a baby, what does that make you?" Lois asked.

"Quiet! Or you both stay home," Mrs. Graves said.

It was after ten when they left the house. The day was sharp and bright, and the wind blew the dried brown leaves along the brick sidewalk next to the Park. Judy noticed that Lois and her mother had that expression on their faces. It was a look they put on every time they went out. An aloof, indifferent look. When they wore it, they never glanced directly at anyone or anything, as though there was something indecent about a direct gaze. Lois wore her coat with the beaver collar and a tiny hat tilted forward on her head. Her kid gloves were immaculate, and she seemed like a delicate miniature of her mother. As they waited for a bus she stood quietly, and when the bus came she helped her mother on. "As though she were a lousy cripple," Judy thought. She resentfully pinched Lois.

"Would you like to sit next to the window, Judy?" Mrs. Graves asked.

"Heavens, no!" Judy exclaimed, her voice polite and amused.

"I'd feel better if you did." Her mother stood holding on to the back of the seat until Judy slid past her. "If you begin to feel funny, let me know and I'll open the window wider."

Mrs. Graves took three dimes from her bag and handed them to Judy. "Here," she said. "You may put them in."

Judy took the money in her slippery fabric glove and one dime dropped to the floor. "How can you be so clumsy?" Mrs. Graves said. She moved her feet to one side. "Do you see it?"

Judy leaned over and her coat pulled at the seams.

The conductor passed down the aisle, clicking his machine and calling, "Fares, please!"

Lois turned around in her seat. "Never a dull moment," she said.

It was some time before Judy found the dime, and her gloves were dusty from the floor. She paid the fares and sat back in her seat, looking out the window, her cheeks crimson.

They got off the bus at Thirty-eighth Street. As they entered the store, Judy took off her coat and carried it. It would not do, she thought, for the saleswoman to see her wearing anything so decidedly un-Continental.

The carpets were soft in the coat department and the place looked sleekly elegant. The girl who came to wait on them was slim and smart in a black silk dress with a lace jabot. Her face lit up when she saw Lois. "Something for this young lady?" she asked.

"Not today," Mrs. Graves answered. "I would like to see the coat you advertised in last Sunday's *Tribune* for this little girl." She rested her hand on Judy's shoulder.

"Oh, yes," the salesgirl said vaguely. She

looked at Judy speculatively. "Well, we'll see. Were you interested in any particular color?"

"Leaf red," Judy said.

The girl went away, and after a time reappeared with a coat hanging over her arm. As she approached, Judy could see the soft gray of a squirrel collar. The girl held up the coat before Judy's dazzled eyes. "This is the one that was advertised, size fourteen."

It was a soft, bright red and the fur collar was even bigger than it had looked in the picture. The back was fitted and the belt that tied in a bow hung below the hem.

"That's it!" Judy cried. "That's the one!"

"Goodness! Not so loud," Mrs. Graves reproved her.

Judy took off her gloves and laid them on the chair. She turned her back to the salesgirl and held her arms stiffly and slipped them into the sleeves. They went in easily at first, but the coat caught above the elbows.

"I was afraid of that," the salesgirl said. "I'm afraid she's a little large for a fourteen."

"Oh," Mrs. Graves said. "Does it come any larger?"

"No," the girl answered. "Size fourteen is the largest we carry on this floor. You'd better try the Junior Misses."

Judy stood with her arms in the coat. She pulled it up and could feel the fur collar around her neck. "Have they one exactly like this?" she asked.

"I really couldn't say," the girl answered.

"Come, Judy," her mother said briskly. "Take it off and we'll look some place else."

Judy pulled at the sleeves and the coat slipped to the floor. The sight of it lying there was more than she could bear, and she stooped quickly and caught it in her arms. "I don't want another coat," she said. "If I can't have this one, I'd rather wear my old coat forever."

She held it close and buried her chin in the fur. Her hard, plump little body was tense.

The salesgirl smiled tolerantly. "It's too bad," she said. "Now, if it were for this young lady . . ." She nodded at Lois.

Lois drew herself up and looked at the girl coldly. "Really, it's not my coat at all. I should think anyone could see that."

She stepped forward and pulled the coat from Judy's arms. "For heaven's sake, turn around and get into this," she said.

Something in her voice lifted the bleakness from Judy's heart. She put her arms back in the sleeves and Lois tugged. The coat went on. It was too tight across the shoulders and it didn't meet by two inches in the front, but it went on.

"Lois," Mrs. Graves said. "It won't do. Have you lost your mind?"

"Anybody would think," Lois told her, pulling the coat into place and tying the belt in a big bow, "that nobody had ever heard of alterations in this family. Besides, it's perfectly silly to think that Judy could wear a junior-miss coat. It would be too old for her. You don't want her to look like her own grandmother, do you?"

"But—" the salesgirl said.

"It would be too old," Lois repeated firmly.

24

"Well," Mrs. Graves said doubtfully.

Lois walked backward and looked at Judy. Her wrists hung awkwardly from the sleeves, the bow caught her in the pit of the stomach, but the fur collar buttoned snugly about her chin and her eyes were shining.

"*I* think it's perfectly charming," Lois said. "Of course, no matter what you put on Judy, she looks as though she were going to you know what."

2

A Furtive Tear

TWO

A Furtive Tear

MRS. GRAVES sighed with relief as she turned the car off the main road and started up the hill. It was well over two hundred miles from New York to South Dorset, Vermont, and she was tired of driving, and tired of listening to her fifteen-year-old daughter Lois, who sat beside her in the front seat, praise the advantages of the new convertible Ford coupés and point out the disadvantages of the Graveses' 1937 Buick sedan. Blankets bulged out of the car's luggage compartment and its gaping cover was held down with a piece of heavy cord. Hilda, the maid, Judy Graves, and her friend Fuffy Adams sat on the back seat, their feet wedged uncomfortably amid a pile of cartons filled with linen and kitchenware.

Mrs. Graves had driven only as far as the toll-gate on the Henry Hudson Parkway when she realized that it had been a mistake to bring Fuffy. There was something about riding in a car that made Fuffy want to sing, and she had sung all the way to Vermont, with Judy and even Hilda joining in. Unfortunately, she had learned most of her songs from her father, a hardened veteran of the first World War, and her choice ranged from "Auprès de Ma Blonde" to "Stand to Your Glasses Steady." At Amenia, Mrs. Graves had suggested that the vocalizers sing some of the Carlton School songs, and Judy and Fuffy obliged with such a vapid rendition of "Brooklet Through the Meadow Dancing" that it was a relief when they went on to an ex-purgated version of "Samuel Hall."

Every summer for fifteen years, Mrs. Graves had driven from New York to the place in South Dorset, and while the contents of the car varied somewhat as the two girls grew older, the trip was always a nightmare. There were no longer nursing bottles, sterilizers, cases of

Walker-Gordon milk packed in ice, gocarts, rubber sheets, and dolls crammed into the back seat, but there were tennis racquets, Lois's golf clubs, Judy's scrapbooks, which she would not leave behind, a game of darts, a badminton set, and a two-quart thermos bottle filled with lukewarm lemonade, from which Judy and Fuffy swilled until the supply was exhausted. Fuffy had bought a milk-chocolate Good Humor before they left the city and had spilled most of it between Mr. Graves' golf bag and the carton that contained the table linen. In spite of the fact that the windows were open, the car smelled of sour milk, moth balls, and, more faintly, of onions—from the hamburgers the travellers had eaten in Sharon.

"One thing," Lois said as the car started up the rutted road that led to their house, "Fuffy's kept Judy's mind off being sick."

"Mmm," Mrs. Graves answered. "Although I thought she seemed a little quiet when we went through Williamstown."

"Look, Fuffy!" Judy exclaimed. "There's

31

George Wade's house. Did you ever see anything like it? They haven't a furnace or anything, and they live there all winter. They throw their cans in the front yard. We can come down and get some if we want them for anything."

"They have lice," Lois said.

"Donald Wade hasn't got lice," Judy said. "He caddies at the club all summer and he bought a bicycle. I like him. He's nice." She pressed her face against the glass of the car window. "Now, when we turn the curve, you can see the poplars across the road from our house. There they are! We're here!"

The house stood on a hill that sloped up from the road. It was a white house with green shutters and was separated from the road by a picket fence, in front of which grew hollyhocks, pink and white phlox, and rambler roses. The roses were in bloom. Mrs. Graves drove up a gravel driveway, past the side porch of the house, and stopped the car at the door of the garage. "Well, that's over," she said.

Judy climbed out of the car, pulling Fuffy with her. "I'm going to show Fuffy the brook, Mom," she said. "And then we'll be right back and help cart in the things."

"Well, *I'm* not going to cart in any things until I've had a cup of tea," Mrs. Graves said.

The brook ran down from the mountains fifty yards from the house. Some of the brush had been cleared away from its banks, and just where the stream reached the road there was a dam which had been built years ago by Mr. Graves when he had decided that anyone could easily make a nice little swimming pool. The dam had never held water, and the pool project had been abandoned. The stones of the dam were covered with soft, wet green moss, and ferns grew in the cracks. The two little girls stood looking down at the clear water. Judy leaned over and spat in it, and they watched the spit until it vanished. "You can see that there's a terrible current," Judy said. "If it was deeper here, it would be dangerous."

"How deep is it?" Fuffy asked.

"Up to my knees in the middle."

They sat down on the grass and Judy let her hand trail in the icy water. "Let's drink like horses," she said.

They leaned forward until their lips touched the clear water and the ends of their hair washed in the stream. They could smell the moist earth and the sodden leaves. Fuffy sat back on her haunches. Her nose and mouth were wet and drops of water trickled down her chin. "It makes my teeth hurt," she said.

Judy, straightening up, paused halfway. "What's that? What's that little thing in that bush? I saw it move."

She parted the leaves. On the ground where the brush was thick lay a baby mouse. It was a pale gray, faintly pink, and it was so still that it seemed to be dead. "I saw it first," Judy said. She touched it softly with her finger. "It's warm. I think we should try to find its pulse."

"I don't think we'd better touch it," Fuffy said. "It might have a fit or something. Besides, its mother probably just left it for a while, and if we move it, she might not be able to find it again."

"I guess that's right. I tell you what. Let's watch, and if she comes back, all right. And if she doesn't come back, we'd better take it to the house and feed it, or it will die."

They backed away silently about three feet and sat without moving. The leaves rustled overhead, and the sounds of the country hummed in their ears. Small gnats flew around their heads, and they could hear the adventurous sound of water rushing over stones. As the minutes passed, they looked at one another with growing excitement. Finally, Judy whispered, "I think she's abandoned it."

"I think so, too."

"Well?"

"Well, I guess we'd better move it."

They crept forward on their hands and knees. "I don't think we should touch it with our hands," Judy said. "I think we'd better make a little litter of a leaf." She picked a sturdy maple leaf and held it beside the mouse. "Push it onto this."

Fuffy prodded with her finger, and the tiny feet stirred and curled. The small body rolled onto the leaf and Judy's hand curved tenderly around it. "Let's put it in our room," she said. "We can make it a little house. And it will get to know us, and when it gets older we can teach it tricks."

"Oh, sure," Fuffy said. "When you get any animal this little, you can do *anything* with it. It will be as tame as a dog."

"We can get it a little collar."

"And a little leash."

"We can take it back to New York in the fall, because by that time it will be housebroken."

Judy's eyes grew soft. "Look at its tiny feet," she said. "They are as *pink!*" A vision of long summer days unfolded before her eyes, days filled entrancingly with the task of raising and training a mouse. They walked toward the house, Judy carrying the leaf, and Fuffy touching the mouse from time to time with a proprietary gesture.

Mrs. Graves and Hilda were in the kitchen unpacking cartons. "Mom," Judy asked, "may we have an empty carton? We found a baby mouse."

Mrs. Graves came over and looked down at the mouse in Judy's hand. "Oh, Judy, you'd better put it back where you found it," she said. "It's too little. It will die."

"No, it won't," Fuffy said hastily. "No, it won't, Mrs. Graves. We're going to feed it, and we won't handle it, *truly*."

"Well," Mrs. Graves said, "you may have a carton, but you mustn't feel too badly if the poor little thing doesn't live."

In Judy's room, Fuffy set the carton on the floor. "I think we should divide it into rooms. A living room, a dining room, a bedroom, and a playroom. We don't need a kitchen, because we can heat its milk downstairs. You get some cardboard for walls and I'll watch the mouse."

Judy laid the mouse gently on her bed. In

37

her father's room, she slipped cardboards out of a few shirts that had been left in a bureau drawer. She found an odd wool sock, a torn handkerchief, and a square china ashtray, and carried these back into her room. "Look," she said, holding out the ashtray. "For its bed. You put in the cardboard and I'll fix its bed. It's probably tired."

It took them almost an hour to fix the house. In the living room was a couch made of part of a safety-match box, a table made of an empty spool, and a chair of folded cardboard; the dining-room table was the top of the match box covered with a bit torn off the handkerchief, while a small puff stool had been made from the rest of the handkerchief; the ashtray was lined with soft wool for a bed and covered with a piece of silk ribbon. "We'll have to buy a little doll's bureau," Judy said. "For its clothes when we make them."

"Let's put him in bed while we heat his milk, and then we can move him into the dining room while he eats it."

"I got the cardboard, so you get the milk," Judy said.

By the time Fuffy came back with the warm milk in a whiskey glass, Judy had made a sign to hang on the door of her room. "Mouse Sanctuary," the sign read, and underneath these letters, which were printed in red crayon, she had written the warning, "Quiet Please! Mouse Sleeping."

They moved the mouse to its soft, padded stool, and Judy dipped her finger in the milk and held it close to the mouse. The tiny animal lay still, its eyes closed. Fuffy rubbed some milk around its mouth, and they waited breathlessly to see if it would reach out with its tongue.

"What shall we name it?" Judy asked.

Fuffy shut her eyes and frowned. "Well, it's a mouse, and it's gray and pink," she said.

"And it's perfectly beautiful," Judy said. "How do you think Pink Beauty would be?"

"I think it would be swell! Pink Beauty! Here, Pink Beauty! Lie down, Pink Beauty! I shouldn't be surprised if he got to be famous."

"Oh, goodness! I shouldn't either! Just think what fun it will be when he gets to know us. I had a kitten that got to know me in a few days. He really did! He almost came when I called him. That is, he would turn around and look at me."

"Oh, Pink Beauty will get to know us, all right." Fuffy's voice was confident. "I'm going to teach him to eat out of a spoon."

"I'm going to teach him to jump through a little hoop."

"I saw a mouse that danced, once. It was a white mouse, and I saw him on Fourteenth Street. He danced and told fortunes."

"Why," Judy said, "they can even teach *fleas* tricks. They can walk a tightrope and climb ladders. I'm going to teach Pink Beauty to walk a tightrope."

They leaned over the box. Pink Beauty lay on the stool, his small mouth wet with milk. He lay very still, and his legs were stretched stiffly out.

"Fuffy!" Judy cried. "He looks funny! Touch him! You touch him!"

40

Fuffy rested her finger gently on one of the small legs. "He feels funny," she said. "Do you think . . ."

They looked at one another in horror. Then Judy picked up the stool and shook the mouse gently into her hand. "It doesn't move," she said. "Pink Beauty doesn't move at all." She got up, holding the mouse in her hand, and walked over toward the window. She turned her head away so that Fuffy could not see her tears. "You wait here," she said. "I'm going to ask my mother."

When Judy had left the room, Fuffy picked up the carton that had been Pink Beauty's house and put it away in the closet. Then, hearing Judy's step once more on the stairs, she walked to the door and waited.

Judy still held the mouse in her hand. "Mom says that he was too little to live," she said. She opened her bureau drawer and searched through the few things she had left behind when she had packed at the end of last summer until she found a white imitation-leather box lined with satin. "My bracelet came in this,"

41

she said. She laid Pink Beauty on the white satin and closed the box.

"Are you going to bury him?" Fuffy asked.

"Of course."

They walked slowly down the stairs and out of the house. Judy led the way across the lawn to a small birch tree that grew close to the white picket fence. "We can dig a place with a stick," she said.

When the hole was deep enough, she lined it with grass and leaves and pressed the white box into it. "I think we should kneel and say the Lord's Prayer," she said. "We don't have to do it out loud."

They knelt on the grass, their lips moving, and then Judy gathered a handful of earth and covered the box. She picked pink buds from the rambler roses and scattered them on the small mound.

"Let's look for a good stone. A nice, flat one," Fuffy said.

Judy and Fuffy walked through the gate out to the road, their eyes serious and their faces solemn. From down the hill came a sound of wheels on gravel, and around the curve rode a boy on a bicycle. He came to a stop beside the two little girls. "Hi, there, Judy," he cried. "I saw you go by in the car."

Judy put out her hand and caught hold of the handlebars of the bike. "Oh, hello, Donald," she said. "This is Fuffy Adams, a friend of mine who's visiting me. This is Donald Wade, the boy I was telling you about. He made the money to buy this bike."

"Oh," Fuffy said. She walked slowly around the bicycle, admiring it. "Can I ride it down the hill?"

"Sure." He stood aside and held the bike steady while Fuffy climbed on.

"I'll bring it right back!" she called. "And then Judy can have a turn!"

Judy stooped down and picked up a stone. It was a soft-gray one and sparkled with a pink light when the sun shone on it. "You wait here," she told Donald Wade, "and I'll be right back."

Under the birch tree, she sat down once more

and scratched at the stone with a pebble. "Pink Beauty," she printed. "Trained Mouse. Died June 7, 1940 A.D." She pressed the stone into the earth, and her hand rested lightly for a moment on the rose-covered mound. Hot tears smarted her eyes. When she heard the crunch of pebbles as Fuffy laboriously pedalled up the hill, she ran to meet her and pushed at her roughly. "My turn, my turn!" she cried.

She wheeled the bike around and started down the hill, pedalling madly and then coasting. The sun was getting lower in the sky, and where the shadows crossed the road the air was cool. The wind blew the hair back from her face and the sound of it filled her ears. By the time she reached the bottom of the hill, her eyes were clear, and there were only faint, dry, salty marks to show where the tears had been.

3

Daddy Dear

THREE

Daddy Dear

Although the picture starring a child actress had been shown in New York at various theatres for almost a year, Judy Graves didn't see it until it reached the small playhouse in her own neighborhood. It was about the hysterical devotion of a curly-haired little girl for her father, a whimsical Englishman who had been lost in the shuffle during the Boer War and had been found again through the untiring efforts of his little daughter and the dignified acquiescence of Queen Victoria. Judy attended the heartbreaking performance on a Saturday afternoon with her best friend, Fuffy Adams, who thought the whole thing bilge and said so. Fuffy was almost thirteen, five months older than Judy, and the years had taken their toll.

47

Judy walked up the aisle of the theatre behind her friend, so that she could compose herself before being exposed to the daylight.

In the lobby, Fuffy turned to her. "I'm gagging," she said.

"Me, too." Judy drew in her breath and swallowed the lump in her throat.

"Did you ever," Fuffy asked, "see anything so absolutely *saccharine*?"

"Revolting," Judy answered. The memory of the child star danced before her eyes; she could see her brave little smile, the blind faith that shone in her face, the cunning way she saluted her father, a soldier of the Queen; Judy could also see her enchanting dresses with their dainty ruffles and the touching mannerisms that softened the heart of every male in the cast.

The two girls left the theatre and walked toward the drugstore on the corner. Fuffy scuffed her feet on the sidewalk in disgust. "The little stinker certainly made a monkey of her old man," she commented.

This was too much for Judy. "Really, Fuff,"

she said, "you shouldn't be so sophisticated. After all, things were different in the olden days. I must say you act awfully hardboiled sometimes."

Fuffy tilted her beret, which bore the emblem of the Carlton School on it, down over one eye. "Well, my old man's a right guy, but if I acted that way around him, he'd slough me."

They hoisted themselves up on the stools in front of the soda counter. They were tall for their twelve years and substantially built. "Make mine a double vanilla with hot fudge," Judy told the man.

"Ditto," Fuffy ordered.

"And no whipped cream on mine," Judy added virtuously.

"I'll have the works."

Seeing that her reproof had sent Fuffy clean off, Judy spoke pacifically. "You've got to admit she acted like a good egg when they put her out of her lovely room at school and made her sleep in the garret."

"Well, yes."

"And she really did find her father, even when everyone thought he was dead."

"Granted," Fuffy said.

Judy took a large spoonful of ice cream. "My father was in the World War," she said thoughtfully, "but he wasn't lost that I know of. Think how you'd feel if we got into another war and your father had to go and was maybe lost somewhere."

"That would be kind of awful," Fuffy agreed.

"So you see how talking the way you do *sounds*," Judy persisted.

"O.K., you win," Fuffy said.

They walked out of the store happily, filled with a pleasing sense of impending disaster. At the entrance to the apartment house where Fuffy lived, Judy gave her an affectionate squeeze. " 'Bye, now," she said.

"Be seeing you," Fuffy responded.

Freed from the chill of Fuffy's skepticism, Judy started toward home. She thought of the careless, almost indifferent way she treated her own father, and her heart melted for him. She remembered how Lois, her fifteen-year-old sister, bossed him, and when she considered the tenderness he had never had from his two daughters, she felt ashamed. Her eyes lighted with a fanatic resolve, and she turned over a new leaf. Elated over the prospect of a future in which she and her father wandered forever hand in hand, she began to skip. Her full cheeks bounced as her feet hit hard on the pavement, and passers-by, seeing her approach, gave her a clear path.

Her thoughts were so filled with a blurred image of her father, who had obligingly donned the uniform of a British officer, that it was rather startling to find him actually sitting in the living room reading a paper when she got home. She walked softly over to his chair and shook her head at him playfully. Her hair hung in a thick, straight line to her shoulders, and no soft curls bobbed about at the movement. "Good evening, Daddy dear," she said.

Mr. Graves lifted his eyes. "Oh, hello there, Lois—Judy," he answered.

She moved closer to him and sat down on the arm of the chair.

"Here, watch what you're doing," he said. He pulled his paper to one side.

"Aren't you home early, Daddy?" she asked.

"Look out now, Judy," he said. "You'll have the arm of the chair off in another minute."

"I've had *such* a lovely day, Daddy. I hope you have, too." She threw a solid little arm around his neck.

"Ouch!" he exclaimed. "Have a heart! Go play with Lois. She's around here somewhere."

"Daddy," she asked, "are you and Mommy going to stay home tonight?"

"Nope," he answered. "And that reminds me that I've got to dress."

He gave her a friendly whack. "Get up."

She pulled herself to her feet and shook her head at him again. "Will you come and say goodbye to me before you go?" In her own mind she was already lying in a small bed in a frilly, old-fashioned nightgown, lifting up her arms for a good-night kiss.

52

"What do you keep shaking your head for?" he demanded. "Have you got something in your ear?"

For a minute she looked at him scornfully. "No," she said. It was an effort to skip toward the door and turn to blow him a kiss.

Mr. Graves walked slowly into the bedroom he shared with his wife. His voice, when he spoke to her, was puzzled. "Listen, Grace, what's got into Judy?"

"Judy?" Mrs. Graves repeated, as though the name were foreign to her.

"Yes," he said. "She acts funny. Nothing you can put your finger on, but just funny."

"You'd better hurry and get dressed or we'll be late," Mrs. Graves told him.

Judy was waiting in the living room when they were ready to leave. She had changed from the sweater and skirt she had been wearing into a last summer's dress of red-and-white dotted swiss with cherry-colored ribbons. It was limp from hanging in the closet and she had had trouble tying the bows, but it had a ruffle around the bottom of the skirt. When she saw her father, she sprang toward him with such enthusiasm that she almost threw him. "How *nice* you look!" she cried.

"Judy!" Mrs. Graves said sternly. "How many times have I told you not to make fun of your father. It's time you girls showed him a little respect."

"Make *fun* of him," Judy repeated in amazement.

"*I* think he looks very nice," Mrs. Graves said. "Now, say good night to him and tell Lois ten-thirty and *no later*. And nine-thirty for you."

She leaned toward Judy and kissed her lightly on the cheek.

Judy caught at her father's arm. "Daddy dear, what are you going to do tomorrow?"

"I'm going to sleep, for one thing."

"All day?"

"All day," he said positively.

"If you should happen to wake up, we might go to the Park." Her dark eyes, as she looked

54

at him, were pleading, and he felt flattered and uncomfortable.

"We'll see," he told her.

Going down in the elevator, Mrs. Graves turned to him. "I think Judy was trying to make amends for poking fun at you," she said. "And I don't think it would hurt you to take her to the Park."

"Tomorrow," Mr. Graves said, "is another day."

The next morning, which was Sunday, Mr. Graves awoke earlier than he had hoped. It was a bright, cold day, and the sun seemed to shine on him reproachfully as he sat in the big chair by the window after breakfast. Judy had been sitting there when he came into the room and had got up to give him her place. Now she lay curled up on the couch across the room and every time he looked at her she gave him a quick, anxious smile.

"Pardon me for interrupting," she said at last, "but if this country goes into the war, would you have to go?"

"I hope not," he answered.

"Oh, I hope so, too. On the other hand, you couldn't very well *not* go, could you? I mean if your regiment went."

"What are you talking about?" he asked crossly. "I don't belong to any regiment."

"You did once."

"Well, *once* I did. And once was enough."

Judy, remembering the gallant way the English father had answered the call to colors, found it hard to answer, "You know best, Daddy dear."

Mr. Graves was conscious of her disapproval and spoke pleasantly. "What time is it?"

She turned her head to see the clock on the mantel. "Almost eleven," she answered.

He rose to his feet. "Well, how about that walk in the Park you promised me?"

"Oh, you *sweet* daddy!" Judy exclaimed. "Wait till I get my things and I'll be with you in a sec. I'll run quick, like a bunny."

Mr. Graves' face, as he took his coat and hat from the hall closet, was a picture.

Although it was very cold, the Park was filled with people; babies looking pink and stuffed sat in their carriages blinking in the sunlight, dogs strained at their leashes and seemed about to choke. Judy clung to her father's arm and skipped by his side.

"Too bad Lois couldn't come," he said. He was remembering the neat way Lois walked.

"Oh, *her*," Judy scoffed. "She went to church."

"That's a very lovely thing for Lois to do. You should have gone with her."

Judy squeezed his arm so hard that he winced. "I'd love to go to church, Daddy, if you would go with me. Shall we?"

"Someday," he said.

As they strolled, Judy talked. "It must be *too* marv to work downtown," she said. "But it must have seemed dull to you at first. I mean, *after*."

"After?"

"After the war. Tell me about the war."

During the next hour, Mr. Graves was thoroughly and not too artfully drawn out. It seemed to him that he had never noticed before how much Judy bounced as she walked or how clumsy she was on her feet. There were times when he was afraid she would fall flat on her face, and he warned her about it. "You'll land on your puss if you're not careful," he said.

They walked all the way around the reservoir. Mr. Graves' arm grew stiff with the weight of Judy's body as she swung on it. By the time they reached the Fifth Avenue exit, he felt as though his side must be worn raw where she had bumped against it. As they stood on the corner waiting for the lights to change, he shook her off. "Stop wiggling, for Christ's sake, and *light!*" he exclaimed. "And step on it, because I'd like to have time to snatch a drink before dinner."

Judy dropped his arm and they started across the street. She stopped skipping and her feet, in their brown oxfords, dragged heavily. It was not usual for her father to mix drinks before Sunday dinner, and the soldier-father in the picture certainly hadn't reached for a bottle after a brief session with his idolized little daughter. As she stumped along, keeping step with her own father, she decided that it was not easy to become the apple of someone's eye. A wave of sadness swept over her, which was immediately followed by a stronger, more familiar sensation. It was a sensation that always made her yawn pleasantly.

Her father looked down at her and smiled. "Well, well," he said. "That must mean somebody's hungry."

4

Madame la Marquise, Toujours Exquise

FOUR

Madame la Marquise, Toujours Exquise

Lois Graves came into the living room and glanced critically at her sister Judy. "Mother," she said, "Judy has her sweater tucked in again."

Without looking up from the magazine she was reading, Judy ran her fingers around the band of her skirt and pulled out her sweater. "Mom, have we any relatives who are employed by Procter and Gamble?" she asked.

"Even if one has the figure for it," Lois went on, "it isn't smart to tuck one's sweater in this year."

"I don't want to have to speak to you about your sweater again," Mrs. Graves said. "Take it out and leave it out."

Judy got up and went over to her mother's chair.

"Well, have we any relatives who are employed by Procter and Gamble?"

Mrs. Graves spread her knitting across her knees and admired it. "Procter and Gamble?" she repeated. "I don't know where you get such outlandish ideas. Why should we have anyone in the family working for *them*?"

"I just wanted to know," Judy said. She left the room with the magazine under her arm and went to the kitchen. Hilda was washing the dinner dishes and the noise was deafening. Judy stood at the door and raised her voice so that it would carry above the sound of the running water. "Hilda, what kind of soap flakes do we use?"

"Don't come in here," Hilda said. "I'm going to mop up the floor in a minute."

"I had no intention of coming in. I merely wanted to know what kind of soap flakes we use."

Hilda glanced at the row of packages on the shelf over the sink. "Ivory, they are."

"Oh!" Judy exclaimed. "That's wonderful! Do you *love* them?"

"Oh, sure," Hilda said. "I'm crazy about them. I use them instead of sugar."

"No, *really*. Can't you think of why you like them?"

"Go away, there's a good girl. I've no time to play."

Judy walked across the room and leaned over Hilda's shoulder to reach for the box of Ivory Flakes. "I'll bring them right back," she promised. "If you would give me the faintest idea why you prefer Ivory Soap Flakes to other brands, I would give you part of my prize money."

Hilda turned off the faucets. "What money?" she asked.

"Well, you see," Judy said, "all you have to do is to write down why you like Ivory Soap Flakes in twenty-five words or less, send it in

65

with the top of the box, and win twenty-five hundred dollars, first prize."

"Oh, one of them things. I never heard of anyone winning one of them."

"The people in this house," Judy said positively, "have absolutely no imagination."

In the room she shared with Lois, she set the magazine and the box of flakes on her bed and took off her bloomers. They were peach-colored rayon ones, a gift from Lois on her twelfth birthday last August. The elastic at the top had been stretched to the breaking point so often around Judy's solid waist that there was no spring left in it. She carried the soap flakes and the bloomers into the bathroom and poured a good handful of the soap into the basin. When she had washed the bloomers, she put them on the radiator to dry. At her desk, she took several pieces of paper and a pencil, and sat down to write. Her thoughts came easily. "I use Ivory Soap Flakes," she wrote, "because as a bride I find them indispensable

66

for my priceless lace wedding veil, an heirloom, and my dainty handmade silk bloomers. They do not fade things either."

Seeing that she had run over her word limit, she crossed out "handmade" and "either." She copied what she had written on the printed form in the magazine, signed it "Mrs. Judith Graves, 36 East 82nd Street, New York City," and enclosed it with the top of the soap box in a small pale-pink envelope.

Once more she read the instructions given in the advertisement. They stated that the prizes would be awarded on the grounds of sincerity, originality of thought, and conciseness. Satisfied that she had scored a hundred on all three counts, she turned the pages of the magazine, looking for more contests. As she began to read, her face was clear and untroubled, but as time passed it took on a worried, apprehensive look.

She walked thoughtfully back to the living room. "Mom, what do you do when your club meets?" she asked.

Mrs. Graves looked up sharply. "My club!" she exclaimed. "What club? I don't belong to any club."

"Oh," Judy said. "Well, a girl at school has a mother who belongs to a club, and they were playing Truth, and they asked one of the women whose wash looked the worst, and she pointed right at this girl's mother."

"That was very rude," Mrs. Graves said. "You'd better be getting ready for bed."

"She made that up." Lois blew on her nails to dry the polish. "I can always tell when she is making up something by the tone of her voice."

"Whether she made it up or not," Mrs. Graves said, "it's a horrid little story. And take that polish off your nails before you go to bed. It's perfectly absurd for a fifteen-year-old girl to paint her nails."

"I did not make it up," Judy contradicted. "It's an absolutely true story."

"Rat whole?" Lois asked.

"Rat whole."

At this sacred verification, Lois sighed. "Well," she said, "anyway, you heard what Mother said about bed."

Back in her own room, Judy undid the top of her plaid skirt and tucked her sweater in. She refastened the skirtband tighter, using a safety pin, which made the front of her skirt bulge alarmingly. Turning on the light over the dresser, she leaned toward the mirror and examined her face. She saw with displeasure the two chicken-pox scars on her forehead, the way her dark-brown eyebrows met in a soft, fuzzy line, and the several small red spots on her cheeks. Her mouth set with determination, and going to the desk, she took out a notebook and wrote in capital letters: "Things to do from now on. 1. Pluck eyebrows. 2. Scrub face with complexion brush and pure Castile soap. 3. Do not eat more than enough to keep healthy. 4. Eat wholewheat bread. 5. Eat no candy except twice a week. 6. Bathe daily. 7. Wash

socks and underwear daily. 8. Do not bite nails.
9. Use jewelry in moderation. 10. Sleep nine
hours every night."

She felt better when the list was finished,
and she tucked it in a cubbyhole which held
other lists. Taking off her two rings, her charm
bracelet, and her locket, she opened the top
drawer of her bureau. It was filled with small
boxes, each one containing a single piece of
finery lovingly wrapped in cotton. The boxes
were all labelled in a cryptic manner: "S. ring
with initials," "Snake bracelet, Aug. 12th, 1938,
A.D.," "Piece of chain?," "Perfume bottle," and
"Lipstick found on floor of Trans-Lux Theatre,
May, 1939." She put the rings, bracelet, and
locket in the boxes reserved for them, closed
the drawer, and began rearranging the things
on the top of her bureau. She set her small blue
enamelled mirror squarely in the centre and
arranged her comb and brush on either side.
Toward the back she placed a large bottle of
pink bath salts, unopened, a bottle of violet
toilet water, a tin penny bank made in the shape

of a suitcase, a stuffed Scottie, an empty bottle of Shalimar, a small tray filled with bobbie pins, and a gilt Easter egg with her name on it; toward the front she set her assortment of glass animals in a neat row.

Fishing into the bottom of the second drawer, she took out a flowered silk nightgown, and after undoing her skirt again, she slid out of her clothes and slipped the nightgown over her head. It had lain in the drawer for two years waiting for an occasion of some sort, and now it was too short, hitting Judy in the middle of her calves, and too tight, pulling uncomfortably across her chest. She seemed unaware of these things and only noticed the beauty of the small pink roses with their yellow centres and the entrancing bit of lace around the neck.

She opened the bath salts, putting the blue ribbon that had been around the top of the bottle away carefully, and went to the bathroom to run her tub. Remembering her resolve about washing her face with a soft complexion brush and pure Castile soap, she laid the nail brush on the edge of the tub before she ran the water, and took off the flowered nightgown.

Her bath was warm and generously scented. For a while she lay on her back, her dark, clear eyes staring rapturously at the ceiling. With one foot she reached for the washcloth and pushed it against the opening to stop the overflow until the water was a bare inch from the top of the tub. Her hands, moving about in the water, looked brown and stubby, and she sat up to scrub them vigorously. Then she soaped the brush again and again, and, beginning at her toes, washed herself all over until the water was thick with suds. Exhausted, she lay back once more, the ends of her straight hair floating at her back. She resolved on a nightly routine of washing, brushing, and grooming herself, and was filled with a sense of wellbeing. Remembering the none too subtle insinuations of the advertisements in the magazine, she grew cold with the thought of how her former carelessness might have ruined her life. It was pleasant in the tub, she admitted, and she felt strangely grown-up lying there spotless and white with the room heavy with steam and the smell of rose geranium.

She heard Lois come into the next room, and she reluctantly got out of the tub and dried herself. It took her over five minutes to brush her teeth with a gentle rotating motion, and then, slipping her flowered nightgown over her head once more, she opened the door to the bedroom.

It seemed cold after the moist warmth of her bath, and Lois looked cool and pretty sitting by her dressing table brushing her hair. With no effort at all, she seemed to have achieved the state of perfection that Judy had set her heart on. "What's the matter?" Lois asked. "What have you got that thing on for? Didn't the laundry come back?"

Without answering, Judy walked toward her and, leaning over, sniffed delicately at Lois's hair. It smelled sweet and rather like the kitten they had in the country last year.

Lois lifted her shoulders. "Go away," she said. "You smell funny."

Judy stepped back, stricken. The flowered

gown swayed against her hard brown legs. "What do you mean, funny?" she asked.

Lois wound a soft curl around one finger. "Oh, you know, funny," she said. "Like soap."

5

For Posterity

FIVE

For Posterity

It was quiet in the living room. Judy Graves sat in the Cogswell chair, staring into space. Her spine rested on the edge of the chair, her feet were stretched stiffly out in front of her, and her hands were folded on the firm mound of her stomach. Mr. Graves lay on the sofa with his eyes closed. The book he had been reading was open face downward on his chest and rose and fell as he breathed. Mrs. Graves moved quietly about the room, a pitcher of water in her hand. She poured a little water into the bowl that held the narcissus bulbs and watched it as it seeped down through the pebbles. "I'm really going to get *in* that hall closet this spring," she said. "I'm going to do it *right*, and not just take things out and put them back again the way I did last year."

"Mom," Judy said, "Fuffy can burp at will. She can do it even when she doesn't have to. She swallows air and does it at will."

Mrs. Graves prodded at one of the bulbs to see if its roots had started. "That's a very disgusting habit, and don't let me catch you trying it."

"I have tried. The air stays down and I sort of swell up. Fuffy did it all this noon, and I thought we'd die."

Mrs. Graves handed the pitcher to Judy. "Take this to the kitchen, like a good girl," she said. "Harry, there's a carton of your stuff on the top shelf. I wish you'd get at it."

Mr. Graves opened his eyes. "There is?" he asked. "What's in it?"

"I'm not quite sure," Mrs. Graves answered. "It's been there since we moved. I marked it with your name. I think it's mostly newspapers and maps."

"I'll get it down Sunday." Mr. Graves picked up his book and began to read.

Judy sat looking at the pitcher in her hand.

78

"What do you want me to do with this?" she asked.

"Put it in the kitchen," her mother repeated.

Judy pulled herself to her feet. "Maybe there's something wonderful in the carton, Daddy," she said. "Something you've forgotten all about. Why don't you open it now?"

"Not tonight," Mrs. Graves said. "I don't want all that mess in here tonight. Haven't you any homework, Judy?"

"Tomorrow's Saturday."

"I know. But I should think you'd like to get it off your mind and not leave it until the last minute."

Judy carried the pitcher to the kitchen and set it on the drainboard by the sink. There was a cake on the table, covered by a painted tin cake cover. She lifted the cover slightly and drew her fingers through the frosting that had run down onto the plate.

"Judy!" Mrs. Graves called. "You're not to eat any more cake!"

"I wasn't going to." She replaced the cover

79

and went into the room she shared with her sister, Lois. Lois sat at the Winthrop desk, a manicure set open on the blotter before her. She held up one hand to Judy, and Judy saw that each nail was painted a different shade.

"Which do you like the best?" Lois asked.

Judy walked over and studied the colors carefully. "The one on your little finger."

"It's the worst one," Lois said. "It's almost purple."

"Well, you asked me."

Lois took a small piece of cotton and moistened it with polish-remover. "Next year," she said, "I'm going to wear polish on my nails no matter what."

"If you do, I will too."

Lois rubbed at her nails. "In a pig's eye," she said.

Judy pulled a straight chair into her closet and climbed up on it. On the shelf under her hats were three scrapbooks. She gathered them in her arms and carried them to her bed. "I haven't the vaguest notion what's in these," she said.

The top one had "Memory Book" printed on the cover with red crayon. On its first page was a picture postal card of the river and bridge in Old Lyme, Connecticut. Judy bent the card and read the message on the other side. "Judy, dear," it said, "There are *eels* in this river! Affectionately, Auntie Julia." Underneath, Judy had written, "In memory of Aunt Julia the time she went to Old Lyme—June—1938."

There were four things pasted on the next page: a tarnished label from a Page & Shaw candy box, with the information "Label from a Page and Shaw candy box given to Mrs. H. L. Graves about 1920. Cost per pound, $1.25. Giver unknown"; a birthday greeting which read, "So you are ten! From your old friend, Mortimer Burroughs"; a card on which was written, "Make those bad old mumps stay on *one* side! And get well soon! Fondest love from Auntie Julia." This was further explained

81

by a notation in Judy's writing, "In memory of the time I had the mumps—November, 1937." The fourth item was a report card, all B's and C's except one A in drawing, which was clarified simply by "In memory of my year in the Sixth Grade—Carlton School."

Judy turned the remaining pages of the book, but they were empty. "I wonder why I didn't keep this up?" she said. "It is very interesting."

The second book had a colored picture of Tyrone Power pasted on its cover. It was half filled with pictures of Mr. Power clipped from movie magazines, and the pictures apparently spoke for themselves, as there was nothing in Judy's handwriting to explain them. "It's funny I don't like him any more," Judy said.

"Like who?"

"Tyrone Power."

"Oh, yes. I remember."

Judy closed the book gently and picked up the third scrapbook. This was covered with a piece of chintz left over from the time Mrs. Graves had made new curtains for the dining room in the country. Against the pale-green background, Judy had printed, "Plays Poems and Stories by Judy Graves Aged 9." There was one play in the book, and Judy lay across the bed as she read it:

1 Scean

Baby in cradle. Mother is sitting beside it. Father comes in.

F) hello.

Mother) Shh Babys just fallen asleep.

F) alright

Jean the daughter comes in.

J) here mother I have the watter from the Brook.

M) Thank you Jean

Baby wakes up.

B) mama

M) Yes dear I'll give you some watter. Give me a glass of watter Jean.

J) hear it is (Baby drinks it

2 Scean

Baby is sick

M) F. get up.

F) What is the matter

M) Baby is sick. Get up and call the nurse.

F) the nurse is ten miles away baby will be dead
when I get back

M) go anyway

F) alright

M) oh dear wake up Jean

J) what do you want

M) Babys sick.

J) oh Baby (she begins to cry.

3 Scean

nurse comes in with father.

M) oh nurse hurry.

J) oh what has she got
nurse examins B.) she has ty.p.

J. faints.

N) where did you get this watter

M) out of the Brook

N) no wonder

B) oh oh mother eeeee

N) shes done for

M) oh (she falls on the crib)

Baby dies

F. falls on the floor. M. follows. Jean is allready
dead.

N) poor family. They all died of T.P.

She leaves

N) I'll have the funerel tomorrow. This is such a bad case. oh dear.
She faints.

Curtain

Judy turned over on her back and stared at the ceiling. "I don't guess you'd really get typhoid fever from the brook in the country, would you?" she asked.

"Of course not," Lois answered. "It comes straight down from the mountain. It's the same water we drink."

"I used to think you could."

Judy got up from the bed and walked over to the desk. "Tomorrow I'm going to sort out all my things and label them. And the ones I can paste in a book, I'm going to. The things that won't go in a book, I'm going to put away in a carton."

Lois held out her left hand. "Now how do you like it?"

"It looks swell. It isn't too purple."

"I'm going to leave it on all night," Lois said.

Judy went back into the living room. Mr.

Graves was still reading and Mrs. Graves was sorting and tearing up letters at the desk.

"Daddy," Judy said, "if you want to get down that carton tonight, I'll help you."

Mr. Graves put his book on the coffee table by the couch. "Well," he said, doubtfully.

"We won't make any mess," Judy told her mother. "Really we won't."

"All right," Mrs. Graves said. "I don't think there's much in it."

Judy followed her father to the hall and watched him as he poked the carton down from the top shelf with a cane. "What do you suppose it can be?" she asked.

"Just junk, mostly." He caught it in his arms as it fell.

Together they carried it into the living room and set it down in the centre of the rug. Mr. Graves took a gold knife from his watch chain and cut the heavy cord. Judy knelt on the floor; her cheeks were pink, and her thick, dark-brown hair fell over her cheeks.

The bottom of the carton was filled with newspapers and road maps, and a few things lay scattered on top: a bunch of keys, a corkscrew, a sleeveless sweater, a pair of worn pigskin gloves, a package of pipe-cleaners, a blue watered-silk tobacco pouch, a steel tape measure, and a small box fastened with a rubber band.

"May I see what's in the little box?" Judy asked.

Mr. Graves lifted the papers out and began to sort them. "Go ahead."

There were three one-cent stamps in the box, a brass padlock, a pair of mother-of-pearl cuff links, and a small gold baseball engraved "1916 —Champions—H. L. Graves." Judy held the baseball in her hand. "This is perfectly adorable," she said. "It would be perfectly adorable on my charm bracelet."

"Don't lose it," Mr. Graves told her.

"Oh, I won't," she promised. "Is that all there is?"

Mr. Graves took the carton and turned it upside down. "That's all," he said.

Judy stood up slowly. "I suppose you must have a lot of things put away somewhere."

"I used to have a lot of stuff," Mr. Graves said, "but I don't know what became of it."

Judy looked down at the things scattered on the rug—the newspapers and maps and the meagre assortment of worn-out things. "What did you get the baseball *for*?"

"We all got one. It was the year we didn't lose a single game."

"Were you very good?"

"I was fair," Mr. Graves said. He went on sorting papers.

Judy went back into her room and sat down on the bed. She picked up the three scrapbooks and held them in her lap. She thought back to the things she had done that week, and further back to the things she had done last summer. The memory was still clear and sharp. She looked down at the small baseball that had lain forgotten in the closet. "Daddy gave me a baseball he won for being champion," she said.

"Did he play baseball?" Lois asked.

"Did he play baseball!" Judy repeated, and

laughed. "He was just champion one year, that's all."

Lois put the manicure things back in their case and started to giggle. "Imagine Dad running around playing baseball!"

"He was champion," Judy said. "I don't see anything very funny in that." She held the baseball tightly in her hand and hugged the scrapbooks closely. She looked around the room at the bright flowered wallpaper, the white ruffled curtains, the familiar maple furniture, and at Lois, who sat at the desk with her hair shining in the light from the lamp. She was sure to remember them always.

"Do you know what I think?" she asked. "I think I'll never forget anything as long as I live."

"Don't be silly," Lois said. She got up and walked toward the bathroom. "I speak for the first bath."

6

The Paragon

SIX

The Paragon

Judy Graves came into the living room and threw herself onto the couch. She still wore her hat and coat, and she pushed her hat back off her forehead and lay staring at the ceiling. On her face was a rapt, dreamy expression, and she seemed entirely unaware of her surroundings.

Mrs. Graves sat on the floor, a small hammer and a box of carpet tacks beside her. She was repairing the bottom of a small upholstered chair, stretching the muslin over the springs and nailing it into place. "Did you have a good time?" she asked. "Now, when you sit in this chair again, Judy, try to be a little careful."

"I had a wonderful time," Judy answered. "Ruth told me she sleeps on the sofa."

"On the sofa?" Mrs. Graves repeated. "How many bedrooms have they?"

"Two. One for Mr. and Mrs. Bates, and one for the boys. Ruth sleeps on the sofa."

Mrs. Graves drove another tack where the strain was the greatest. "Oh," she said. "That must be inconvenient. What do Mr. and Mrs. Bates do when they want to sit up late?"

"They don't sit up late," Judy explained. "They all go to bed at the same time."

"Nonsense!" her mother exclaimed. "Mr. and Mrs. Bates can't go to bed when their children do every night."

"But they do," Judy insisted. "You see, they have rules."

"They must have." Mrs. Graves stood up and turned the chair back in place.

"The boys have a double-decker bed," Judy said. "I wish Lois and I had one, and I could take the top bunk. The boys' room is small and there isn't room for two beds."

She sat up on the couch and struggled out of her coat. It fell to the floor and she lay back again, her hat mashed against a cushion.

"You and Lois are very lucky girls to have such a nice big room," Mrs. Graves told her.

"The boys' room is lovely. Everything is built in. They have a toy box built in under the window, and shelves, and drawers built in the closet. It was Mrs. Bates' idea. She's the one who thought up the rules, too."

"Did you have a nice lunch?" Mrs. Graves asked.

"We had a wonderful lunch. We got it ourselves. At least, Ruth and I did most of it, and Mrs. Bates made the salad dressing. She put some chili sauce in some mayonnaise and it was terribly good. We washed the dishes, too, while Mrs. Bates read to us. She reads aloud an hour every day. After lunch and after dinner."

"Well," Mrs. Graves said doubtfully, "that must be very nice."

"She can do anything. She's hooking a rug. Ruth and I worked on it while Mrs. Bates was having her nap."

95

"Good heavens!" Mrs. Graves exclaimed. She picked up the hammer and the box of tacks.

"She has to take a nap," Judy said, "because she gets up at six every morning, and she has everything done by ten."

"Well, if you're not too tired, you'd better hang up your coat and hat." Mrs. Graves' voice had a slightly acid tone.

Judy sat up on the couch and stooped down to get her coat. A button had come loose, and she twisted the thread to tighten it. When she saw the hammer in her mother's hand, her face brightened. "Mrs. Bates made a dressing table with little skirts on it out of an old kitchen table," she said. "Maybe you could make one. The whole thing only cost her about a dollar."

"I doubt if I could," her mother answered. "You'd better get washed up." She went to put the hammer and tacks away in the kitchen.

Judy walked into her room, swinging her coat. She took a wooden hanger from the pole in her closet and looked at it distastefully. "You can buy coat hangers covered in chintz," she called to her mother, who was walking across the hall. As Judy put her coat away in the closet one of her dresses fell to the floor, but she did not notice. She walked over to her bureau and studied the litter of small things that covered its top. She went to her mother's bedroom, opened the door of the closet, and took down an empty hatbox. "May I have this old hatbox?" she asked.

Mrs. Graves was in the bathroom washing her hands. She turned off the water when Judy spoke. "What do you want it for?"

"For some things. All you really need on a bureau is a comb and a brush and a mirror."

Going back to her own room, Judy put the box on the floor and packed the small glass and china animals that marched across the bureau neatly into it. Her toilet water and the perfume bottle she put in the top drawer, and then she arranged her comb and brush in the centre of the scarf. Her bedroom slippers still lay on the floor by the bed where she had slipped them off, and she kicked them under the flounce of the spread. She hung up a skirt that lay on a chair, and cleaned off the top of the desk, and sat down to write.

"7 A.M." she wrote. "Get up. 7 A.M. to 7:15 A.M. Wash and brush teeth. 7:15 A.M. to 7:30 A.M. Get dressed."

Judy stopped and looked thoughtfully out of the window. The Graveses had breakfast at eight, and it had been her habit to lie in bed luxuriously until ten minutes of eight and then to wash hurriedly and slip into her clothes. She was left with a full half-hour on her hands. "7:30 A.M. to 8 A.M. Fool around," she put down. "8 A.M. to 8:30 A.M. Eat. 8:30 A.M. Go to school."

It suddenly occurred to her that she would have to make a different schedule for Saturday and Sunday, and she decided to finish it later. She wandered back into the living room and found her mother seated in the chair by the window, putting the final touches to a sweater. Judy sat down on the window sill to watch her. "Do we have balanced meals?" she asked.

"Mrs. Bates balances her meals so that everyone gets everything, like iron and roughage."

"I suppose so," her mother answered.

"They have supper at night. Mrs. Bates says that your big meal should be in the middle of the day. Ruth and the boys come home from school and have a hot lunch. A dinner, really. And at night they have cocoa and toast and fruit. I think that's a very sound idea, don't you?"

"I do not," Mrs. Graves said positively. "When does Mr. Bates get fed? Or doesn't he?"

"Oh, I suppose he eats downtown," Judy told her. "Mrs. Bates says he's wonderful with the children. He helps them with their homework."

Mrs. Graves looked up at Judy and her face was puzzled. "Do you want Daddy to help you with your homework?" she asked.

"I'll say I don't," Judy answered. "Daddy gets mad. They want me to come over tomorrow afternoon," she went on. "They are going to paint the wicker chairs. So may I, *please?*"

"I don't think you ought to be cooped up all Sunday afternoon with the smell of wet paint," Mrs. Graves said. "I think you'd better play with Fuffy in the Park."

There were four sharp rings of the doorbell, and Judy sprang to her feet.

"It's Lois!" she exclaimed. "I'll let her in."

She ran to the door and opened it. "Lois," she said, "will you teach me how to knit?"

Lois carried her skates over her arm, and her short corduroy skirt was up to her knees. "I will not," she said firmly.

"You ought to see Ruth Bates knit," Judy told her. "Her mother taught her. Her mother knits like a professional, and Ruth made herself a whole dress."

Lois put her skates away and walked into the living room. "Ruth Bates!" she said. "That weasel!"

"You don't know her," Judy said. "You don't know anything about her at all. Lois, would you like a double-decker bed?"

Lois turned to stare at her. "And have you

snorting and turning over my head?" she asked. "I should say not."

Judy, deflated, went slowly back to the room she shared with Lois and sat down at the desk. She took out the list she had started and set to work. She worked until dinner was ready, and by that time had successfully accounted for every minute of her week. She was silent at the table and only commented once on the food. "Squash has a funny taste. We had carrots and peas for lunch," she said. "They were terribly good."

After dinner, when Hilda had carried the plates into the kitchen, Judy thought reminiscently of washing the lunch dishes, and of how the warm suds had felt on her hands, and of the sound of Mrs. Bates' voice as she read. She remembered how surprised Mrs. Bates was when the dishes were finished, and the good feeling that had warmed her as she washed the dish towel. She stood at the door of the kitchen and watched Hilda splashing away at the sink. Hilda looked busy and important. Judy wondered what the Bateses were doing now, and pictured Mrs. Bates sitting in the kitchen chair reading to Ruth and the boys while Mr. Bates worked away at some small allotted task in the background.

She started back to her room and looked in the living room as she passed. Her father was reading, her mother was knitting, and Lois sat at the desk copying names and numbers in her new address book. The lack of community spirit depressed Judy, and she resolved that she would ask her mother again in the morning if she could help paint chairs at the Bateses'. In her room she took a book from the shelf and lay across the bed to read. It was a book about a mother and father who had a large family of children.

The next day it seemed as though Sunday dinner would never be over, and that she would never get to the Bateses' house. It was after two when she was ready to leave, and her mother came to the door to say goodbye. "Now, don't think you have to stay and paint the chairs if the smell of paint makes you feel funny," Mrs. Graves said.

"Oh, I love to paint," Judy assured her.

She almost ran the three blocks to the Bateses' apartment, and when Ruth opened the door, Judy was breathless. Mrs. Bates was sitting in the chair in the kitchen, just as Judy had imagined her last night, and Mr. Bates and the boys were clearing the table. "I'll help wash!" Judy cried, and throwing her coat and hat onto a chair, she hurried to the sink and plunged her hands into the warm, white suds.

It was nearly six o'clock when she got home. She slammed the front door shut, raced into the living room, and bent down to kiss her mother. Her cheeks were red and cold, and her hair smelled of the outdoors. "Well, how was the painting?" Mrs. Graves asked.

"It was all right," Judy said. "I didn't paint very long. We got paint on the rug and Mr. Bates didn't like it. I didn't care. It isn't much fun painting wicker furniture, because it doesn't show."

Mrs. Graves kissed her again. "How was Mrs. Bates?" she asked.

"Oh, she was all right. I helped with the dishes, and there were an awful lot of them, and Mrs. Bates didn't read such an interesting book as she did yesterday. Ruth asked if we had a maid, and I said of course we did. And she said it must be wonderful to have a maid."

Mrs. Graves took one of Judy's hands and held it against her cheek. It smelled faintly of soap and dishwater.

"When we stopped painting, I went over to Fuffy's," Judy said. "We've been out in the Park. We were talking to an old man who sells peanuts. He's very poor, he said, and so we told him we would start a campaign and raise some money so he can have his teeth fixed."

She pulled away from her mother and started for her room. "I'm going to put down the names of everybody we know, and how much they should give," she said.

Mrs. Graves looked after her and smiled.

She got up and went to her room and took twenty-five cents from her pocketbook. Judy was busy writing at her desk, and Mrs. Graves laid the money on the blotter. "You can put me down for a quarter," she said.

7

The Best Things Come
in Small Packages

SEVEN

The Best Things Come in Small Packages

DINNER on Christmas Eve was a tasteless affair, and it was a relief to everyone when it was over. Judy Graves even forgot to ask if she could pick up her lamb chop to eat it, and she cut the meat from the bone and pushed the pieces indifferently around her plate with a fork. The feeling of anticipation that had carried her lightly along for the past two weeks had suddenly become concentrated and had settled like a cold, heavy weight in her stomach. She swallowed the last of her milk in a gulp. "I'll help Daddy bring the tree down," she offered.

Mr. Graves pushed back his chair. "Yes," he said, "we might as well get started."

109

The tree had been selected three days before and carried to a corner of the apartment-house roof so that it would keep fresh in the cold air. Lois and her mother had carefully chosen it for its shape. Now, as Mr. Graves and Judy left the table, Lois spoke. "It isn't so awfully *big*. I mean it's not one of those mammoth things that Daddy usually gets, but it's nice and thick and a *lovely* shape. You'll see what I mean when it's set up."

There were a dozen or more trees on the roof. The air smelled of them. Judy hopefully glanced at the tag on the tallest one. "I don't think this is it," she said. "This one has a long name on it."

At the end of the row, in a corner protected from the wind, a small tree lay against the railing, its branches tied with string. "This must be it," Judy said. She pulled it upright and it swayed toward her. The top branches touched her cheek and the scent of it filled her nostrils. She put her arms around it and held it close. "It isn't so very big," she said, defiantly, "but

110

it's a beautiful little tree. A perfectly *beautiful* little tree. I'll carry it."

They walked back toward the elevator.

Lois was waiting for them by the door, and she looked anxious. "It's *darling*," Judy told her quickly. "It isn't small at all. There were some larger trees on the roof, but they looked scrawny. *Really.*"

She carried the tree to the living room and laid it on the clean sheet that had been spread between the windows. Her hands were sticky from the sap and dark green needles clung to her sweater.

Lois's face lost its anxious look. She had slipped a smock over her dress and it gave her an efficient appearance. "I have sort of an idea," she said. "I think it might be unusual if we picked out just blue and silver ornaments and did the whole thing in blue and silver. I mean, there would be plenty of them because the tree is so much smaller."

"Not use all the ornaments!" Judy exclaimed. "You're nuts!"

111

"Oh," Mrs. Graves protested, "I think it would be better to use all the ornaments. We always have, and I'm fond of them."

"Really," Lois said, "you all act like a lot of reactionaries. You just won't listen to any new suggestions, *ever*."

Mr. Graves fastened the tree in its stand and cut the string from the branches. "I'll tell you what," he said. "When you're eighteen, Lois, you can trim the tree the way you want it, and when Judy's eighteen, she can trim it the way she wants it. How's that?"

He walked over to the table where the Christmas-tree ornaments lay in their boxes. Deliberately he chose a red-and-gold striped ball and hung it on the tree. His action stripped the authority from Lois and her smock and lifted the apprehension from Judy's heart.

"I'm going to put the cat face on for my first one," she said.

It took them over an hour to trim the tree and arrange the crèche on strips of cotton underneath it. Judy, kneeling to set a small celluloid reindeer near a tiny pine tree, suddenly remembered last year and how Bilgy, the cat that had died last summer, had knocked the whole scene over after they had arranged it. Her eyes smarted with tears and she shook her hair over to hide her face.

"It does seem strange without one single toy," Mrs. Graves said sadly. "It really looks bare without any toys under the tree."

"Speaking of toys—" Lois stopped abruptly and giggled.

"Speaking of toys what?" Judy asked.

"Oh, nothing," Lois told her. "You're too old for toys, of course."

"When I was twelve," Mrs. Graves said, "I was still playing with dolls."

"Dolls!" Lois exclaimed. "Oh, Mother!"

"It's living in New York," Mr. Graves said. "And that fool school."

"Well, get your stockings out, girls, and let's hang them," Mrs. Graves put in hurriedly.

Lois's stocking was silk and slim, with a small foot, and Judy brought a wool knee-length sock

113

with a darn in the toe. "Turn your back, Judy," Lois said. She slipped a small package into the toe of Judy's sock.

"Just weight them with the candlesticks," Mrs. Graves told them. "I'll fix them later."

She went to her room and came back with her arms full of packages. "No poking at these," she said.

The Cogswell chair was for Judy's things, the wing chair for Lois's, and the couch for Mr. and Mrs. Graves' presents. Until this year Judy's chair had been almost empty, as her toys had been arranged under the tree after she had gone to bed. This year her chair looked the same as Lois's. Judy, glancing at the packages, wondered if the biggest one could be the jade-green lounging pajamas.

She got the gifts for her father, mother, and Lois from the shelf in her closet. She had bought her father a gadget called a Scotch Bartender, which measured an exact jigger of whiskey, and a practical and charming present for her mother. It was an ashtray, and attached to it was a frog's head. You inserted a cigarette in a place in the mouth, and the ashes fell in the tray. A silk-covered rubber tube extended from the inside of the frog's head and ended in a dainty amber cigarette holder. The idea of the whole thing was to be able to smoke in bed without fear of dropping ashes on the blankets and perhaps going up in flames. For Lois, she had bought a pair of red gloves fastened at the back with a gilt Christmas bell. She had wrapped her packages with care and covered them with stickers that called out, "Season's Greetings," "Joyeux Noël," "Merry Christmas," or warned, "Do Not Open Until Christmas" and "Hands Off Until Dec. 25th."

Lois had wrapped her gifts in blue cellophane and tied them with silver ribbon. Her stickers were silver stars.

It was almost midnight by the time the room was straightened and the carols were sung. Activity had thawed the lump in Judy's stomach somewhat, and she was surprised to find that she was a little sleepy. "I'll never close an eye," she said.

When Lois and Judy were in bed, Mrs. Graves came in to kiss them good night. "I never can realize that you two will never believe in Santa Claus again," she sighed.

"Judy pretended she did until she was almost *eight*," Lois said.

"I did not."

"I beg to differ."

Mrs. Graves uncurled Judy's fingers. "You didn't even wash."

"I did," Judy said, "all but this hand. That isn't dirt, it's sap and it smells good."

She turned on her side and snapped out the light over her bed. For almost five minutes, it seemed as though morning would never come.

The next thing Judy knew, it had come and gone in a swirl of white tissue paper, red ribbons, excited exclamations, and kisses. The big package had contained the jade-green lounging pajamas, which were a little too short and had

116

to be exchanged. There were six pairs of silk stockings of a new shade called Woodsmoke, a pair of pink silk pants with lace edges, a silk nightgown that trailed on the floor, monogrammed writing paper, a new charm bracelet with fourteen charms on it, a bottle of 4711 eau de cologne, white kid gloves that fastened with a zipper, a tiny bottle of real perfume (lily of the valley), bedroom slippers with white fur tops, and, from Lois, a blue satin stocking box. The big present, of course, was the lounging pajamas, but the thing that Lois had tucked in the toe of her stocking was the funniest; it was a small crib with twin dolls in it, bought from the five-and-ten. The dolls were wrapped in tiny cheap blue blankets. Judy screamed with laughter when she saw it.

"That's why," Lois explained, "I very nearly died when Mother said what she did about toys last night."

"I don't wonder," Judy answered. She set the crib under the tree. "There, Mother, that should make you feel better."

She arranged her presents carefully in her chair. "I think I'll go over and give Fuffy hers," she said. Fuffy was her best friend and lived two blocks away.

In her room, she took off her wool socks and slid her new silk stockings over her legs. They felt strange and cold, and her shoes, when she put them on, slid up and down at the heels. Although her knees were plump, the stockings wrinkled around them and she had trouble keeping them up. She put on her new white gloves, her charm bracelet, scented a clean handkerchief with a drop of the lily-of-the-valley perfume, and started toward Fuffy's house. She held the package stiffly, as her hands were pinched in the new gloves. Halfway down the block she met Fuffy. One glance told her that Fuffy was wearing silk stockings, and though Fuffy wore her old wool mittens, Judy could see the peach-colored collar of a new blouse showing over the top of her double-breasted coat. Fuffy was also carrying a package, identical in shape with the one Judy held. She pressed it into Judy's arms. "Here," she said. "Merry Christmas."

"Same to you," Judy replied. "And here."

They walked toward the corner and stood by a large metal basket, into which they carefully threw the tissue-paper wrappings. "I got yours green," Judy said.

"I got yours red, *naturally*."

They had given one another pocketbooks of colored imitation leather, handsomely outfitted with lipstick, powder and rouge compact, comb, and cigarette case.

"I *love* mine," Fuffy said.

"Me, too."

They swung the pocketbooks over their arms and started toward the Park. The streets were alive with children—little children in bright woollen snow suits, five- to ten-year-olds whizzing by on skates and scooters. There were mere babies pushing toys with bells that rang as the wheels turned or riding in shiny red

119

wagons. Smug little girls wheeled English coaches and fussed with dolls' blankets. Judy dangled her charm bracelet. "Look," she said.

They stopped while Fuffy admired the charms. "Oh, a little ice pick and a pair of tongs! And a lantern and a wheelbarrow! Honestly, it's absolutely the cutest one I've ever seen!"

"Daddy picked it out all by himself," Judy told her. There was pride in her voice, as though she were speaking of a backward child who had suddenly and amazingly refused to fit a square peg into a round hole.

They talked about what they had received. As they had made almost identical lists during recess at school, the conversation lacked variety.

"Goodness," Judy said, dodging a little girl on roller skates, "it's as much as your life's worth to walk on the street today!"

"Remember when you got the little automobile?" Fuffy asked. Her eyes were wistful. "I don't think I ever had as much fun any Christmas as the year you got that automobile. It was the year I got my Pogo stick."

"The way we tore around in it!" Judy smiled tolerantly. "I was late for dinner."

"How old were we when we got our tricycles?"

"Oh, we must have been *little*," Judy answered. "Five or six, I guess."

"I remember it perfectly."

They tacitly avoided walking in the Park and stayed on Fifth Avenue. The air was filled with the noises children make: screams, whistles, the sound of wheels on cement, the soft thud of balls, and laughter so shrill and mirthless that it could be heard over all the other sounds. Judy's hands grew cold in her new gloves and the seams of her stockings twisted on her legs. They walked on and on, waiting sedately at corners for the lights to change, swinging their new bags from their arms. At Sixtieth Street they started back uptown. Judy's heels hurt where her shoes had rubbed against them and several times Fuffy stopped to adjust her stockings.

By the time they had reached the door to Fuffy's apartment on Seventy-ninth Street, they had grown silent. "Well, Merry Christmas *encore*, and thanks loads for the bag," Judy said.

Judy was surprised to see that it was not even noon when she reached home. The apartment was silent. Lois and her mother had gone out and her father lay on the living-room couch, asleep.

She took off her coat and hat and hung them in the hall closet and went into the living room. The little tree stood between the windows, heavy with ornaments. In the daylight it looked overburdened, as though its branches were not strong enough to carry the weight of so many things. She began rearranging her presents. There didn't seem to be so many now; the gloves were in her coat pocket, she was wearing the bracelet and one of the pairs of stockings, and she had taken the perfume to her room. She decided to put her things away and found that she could easily make them into one load. She put the stocking box Lois had given her in her bureau drawer and arranged the stockings in the compartments. Her new nightgown and silk

122

pants she spread over the top of her old underwear.

Closing the drawer, she left the rest of her things lying on the bed and walked back to the living room. For a while she stood looking out of the window, jingling her bracelet against the glass. Then she walked over to the tree once more. Stooping down, she picked up the little crib with the twin babies. And then she sank to the floor. She could almost get under the lowest branches of the tree by ducking, and she edged closer to it.

Bits of silver rain touched her hair and the boughs overhead gave her a closed-in feeling, like being in a small house. She put the crib in her lap and unpinned the blankets, smoothed them out, and pinned them more tightly under the babies' chins. "Go to sleep," she said softly, and rocked the cradle lightly with her finger.

8

New Leaf

EIGHT

New Leaf

Because both Judy and Lois Graves had stayed awake to see the New Year in and their mother and father had been to a party that didn't even get under way until almost midnight, breakfast was unusually late on New Year's Day. Mr. Graves, after hurriedly drinking a large glass of orange juice, had settled into his chair at the head of the table in a manner that suggested a minor collapse, while Mrs. Graves, toying with a toasted English muffin, had a harassed look. "Would you rather have a cup of cocoa or a glass of milk instead of that coffee, Harry?" she asked.

Mr. Graves glanced at Judy, who was scooping spoonfuls of marmalade onto her muffin,

127

and pushed his chair back from the table. "No," he said. "Thanks just the same."

Lois picked up a crisp piece of bacon from her plate and bit into it daintily. "I love late breakfasts," she said. "I think we should have them every Sunday and every holiday. I'm always hungrier in the morning on Sundays and holidays. And you could have wonderful things to eat. Like the English. Sausages, creamed haddock, kidney stews, all kinds of eggs and stuff. I've read about how they do."

Mrs. Graves looked nervously at her husband. "When you girls finish eating, it might be nice if you took a good long walk in the Park to blow the sleep out of your eyes."

"I'm not sleepy," Judy said. "I'm not sleepy at all. I feel swell. And, besides, I want Daddy to tell us about the surprise."

"What surprise?" Mr. Graves asked.

"The surprise you were talking about last night," Judy said. "Don't you remember? After we finished the champagne. Mmmm!" She closed her eyes and licked her lips reminiscently. "Champagne is wonderful. It's as good as ginger ale. I didn't even feel mine and I had half a cocktail glass full."

"You feel it the next day," Lois said. "After you drink a lot of water. Uncle Ed told me so."

"Your Uncle Ed is a very foolish young man," Mrs. Graves said severely. "And you mustn't believe everything he tells you."

Judy picked up her glass of water and drained it. "I'm going to try it anyway," she said. "I think Lois felt hers. She let me have the tub first. Drink all your water, Lois, and see what happens."

"Girls!" Mrs. Graves exclaimed. "You're acting very, very silly. Now stop your nonsense, and maybe Daddy will tell you about the surprise."

Judy watched Lois as she drank her glass of water. "Yes, go on, Daddy," she said.

Mr. Graves looked at the bright flushed faces of his two daughters and took a small sip of coffee. "Well—" he began.

"It was about the idea you had," Mrs. Graves

prompted him. "The idea of letting them handle their own money."

"Money!" Judy repeated. "Oh, boy!"

"That's right," Mr. Graves said. "That's right, it was."

"Perhaps *I'd* better explain," Mrs. Graves said. She raised her eyebrows slightly. "You see, girls, your father thought that if he gave you an allowance that was *more* than you needed for lunches and spending money, it would teach you to *save*. I mean save up for birthday presents, Christmas presents, and things of that sort."

"I think I ought to get more than Judy," Lois said. "I'm older."

"What's that got to do with it?" Judy asked. "I'm under *just* as heavy expense."

"If there's any quarrelling," Mrs. Graves said, "we won't discuss it any more."

"O.K.," Lois said.

"Well," Mrs. Graves went on, "your father thought of five dollars a week each. Now, say you spend thirty cents a day for lunch at school.

That's five times thirty, and that's fifteen. A dollar and fifty cents. And that leaves you, let's see . . ." She closed her eyes and frowned. "How much does that leave, Harry?"

"Three-fifty."

"Three-fifty," Mrs. Graves repeated. "And counting out another dollar and a half for movies and sodas, you'd still have two dollars left. And two dollars a week for fifty-two weeks is ——"

"One hundred and four dollars," Mr. Graves said.

"Golly!" Judy cried. "One hundred and four dollars! You could buy almost anything for that."

"Yes," Lois said. "But remember Christmas presents. I spent almost ten dollars on Christmas just for the family and Hilda. Not that I *minded.*"

"That still leaves ninety-four dollars," Judy said.

"And birthdays," Lois went on. "I give to you three and Hilda in this very house, and I give to Joan, and Barbara, and—and Mary, and goodness knows how many cards I send."

"Even so," Judy said. "One hundred and four dollars. And if you didn't go to the movies so much, you could make it lots more." She got up from the table swiftly and threw her arms around her father. "I never heard of anything so wonderful! What made you think of it?"

"God knows!" said Mr. Graves.

Judy pressed her cheek against his. "You're just pretending," she whispered. "You did it for the New Year. I *know*."

"When do we begin?" Lois asked eagerly. "Today?"

"I think today would be a very *good* day to begin," Mrs. Graves said. "And then you two girls could go to your room and draw up a budget. Why don't you give them their money now, Harry?"

Mr. Graves got up slowly from his chair and went to his room. His feet, in their leather mules, made a soft, swishing sound as he walked. In a few minutes he came back into the dining room, some crumpled bills in his hand. "Here's eight dollars," he said.

"Did you look in your overcoat pocket?" Mrs. Graves asked.

"Yep," he said. "That's where I found this. I didn't have anything in my wallet. Must have put this in my overcoat after I paid the taxi."

Mrs. Graves arose. "I might have a little something," she said. "Although I marketed for over the holiday. We're having turkey again." She rustled out of the room and returned with a dollar bill.

"Well, that makes it nine," Judy said hopefully. "Maybe Hilda has a dollar."

"Of course, you *could* wait for the rest until tomorrow," Mrs. Graves said.

Mr. Graves, catching sight of Judy's face, said that maybe Hilda might have a dollar. "I can cash a check at the club. Do me good to get out in the air."

Mrs. Graves stepped on the buzzer under the table, and when Hilda opened the swinging door that led to the kitchen, she said brightly,

"Oh, Hilda! Hilda, I wonder if you have a dollar you can let the girls have until Mr. Graves cashes a check. They're planning to turn over a new leaf and start off the new year on a budget. And they can't wait to get started, it seems." She laughed tolerantly.

"I have a dollar right here, Mrs. Graves," Hilda said. "I always carry it pinned to the inside of—well, pinned to the inside, in case I lose my pocketbook."

She turned her back to them and fumbled with the collar of her dress. She brought out a folded bill and handed it to Mrs. Graves.

"That's fine, Hilda," Mr. Graves said. "I'll take care of the interest."

"Don't mention it, I'm sure," Hilda answered, her voice prim.

"Now then, here you are," Mr. Graves said. "Five dollars for Lois and five dollars for Judy."

He handed a five-dollar bill to Lois and five one-dollar bills to Judy.

"Thanks *ever* so much," Judy said. "Come on, Lois, let's do our budgets."

"I have to get dressed first," Lois said. "And then I think I'll go over to Joan's and tell her. I'm going to think about mine."

"I'm going to do mine *now*," Judy said.

In her room, Judy sat down at her desk, and took out a pad of paper and a pencil, and printed "BUDGET" at the head of the page. Then, after a few minutes, she wrote, "Item 1— Lunches for 5 days at 30 cents per lunch— $1.50." Hearing Lois come into the room, she asked, "Do you always take the thirty-cent lunch?"

"Almost always," Lois said. "Except when I'm reducing."

Judy tore the piece of paper from the pad and threw it into the scrap basket. "I think I'll reduce," she said. "I'll save a quarter a week right off the bat."

She wrote "BUDGET" again, and then, "Item 1 —Lunches for 5 days at 25 cents per lunch— $1.25." Her hair fell across her cheeks as she leaned over the desk. "Item 2—Movies—1 movie a week at 55 cents per movie—55 cents.

Item 3—Missilaneous—sodas, candy and other excessories at 10 cents per day—70 cents." She added up the total and put down, "Total Expenses—$2.50."

"Look, Lois," she said excitedly. "I've put down everything I can possibly think of and I still have two dollars and fifty cents left every week. Let's see, that makes—why, that makes one hundred and thirty dollars a year!"

"Do you know what I'm going to do?" Lois asked. "I'm going to save everything I can for three years and then I'm going to Bermuda. I'll be eighteen, and there is absolutely no reason why you can't go to Bermuda alone when you're eighteen."

"Bermuda!" Judy cried. "That's a wonderful idea. What's it like?"

"It's tropical," Lois said. "And everyone rides bicycles because there are no automobiles allowed, and you can go swimming every day, and play tennis, and ride horseback, and wear perfectly stunning cruise clothes."

"Well, I'm going to save for something like

that, too," Judy said. "Only I may go West to a dude ranch and buy some perfectly stunning cowboy boots and a perfectly stunning saddle." She stared at the pad of paper, excitement mounting in her. "That's *exactly* what I'm going to do. I'm going West and stay all vacation and train for a rodeo. Then, when I get good enough, I can make scads of money in prizes. I'm going to put down every nickel I spend and put it on a debit side, and every nickel I save I'll put on a credit side. You haven't got a book with a line down the middle, have you?"

"No, I haven't," Lois said. "What difference does it make? You can draw one."

"It won't look right. I think I'll go down to the stationery store and see if they have one. I'm going to keep my accounts *perfect*." She got up and went to the closet to get her coat with the fur collar. "I wish I had a billfold," she said. "I sort of hate to crumple all that money up in my little change purse." She put on her coat and hat and took her small red handbag from the top of the bureau. The five one-dollar bills were lying on the desk, and she tucked them into her purse. "I'm going to carry it all, just in *case*."

Lois pulled one silk stocking up over her leg and straightened the seam. "Well, see you next week," she said.

"What do you mean 'See you next week'?"

"Oh, you and all that money."

Judy's laugh was assured. "You're nuts," she said.

The stationery store was small and still crowded with unsold Christmas toys. There were cheap little trains that could be wound up with a key to run on miniature tracks, dolls whose dresses were not quite fresh, a box of soiled Christmas and New Year cards, mechanical toys, racks of magazines, and, on top of the cigar counter, a handsome selection of five-cent candy bars. The place smelled of cigar smoke, library paste, and printer's ink. Judy walked in and leaned her elbows on the counter. "Good morning, Mr. Epstein," she called.

From the back of the store, a small, studious-looking man appeared. He wore a dark-brown sweater to guard himself against the drafts that blew across the shop every time the door was opened. "Happy New Year, Judy," he said.

"Oh, I forgot. Happy New Year to you, Mr. Epstein. Have you sort of an account book like you keep budgets in, with a line down the middle? A red line."

"Like a ledger," he said. "I see." He rummaged among the pads, notebooks, and boxes of writing paper in the case in back of the counter and brought out a large gray book on which the word "Ledger" was printed in italics. "How's this?" he asked.

Judy opened the book. There was not only a red line down the middle of every page but red lines that separated the dollars from the cents.

"It's perfect," she said. "How much is it?"

"Fifty cents."

"Well," Judy said. "Fifty cents is quite a lot, but it's perfect and I can use it for years. You see, I'm on an allowance now, a real *allowance*, not just lunch money and fifteen cents a day. And I've figured everything out, and I'm going to save two dollars and fifty cents every week. I'm going to put it in a bank so I can't *touch* it, not for *anything*."

"A bank?" Mr. Epstein said. "You should have one of those banks like a cash register. I had a few here at Christmas." He came out from behind the counter and looked in the showcase on the other side of the room. "Here you are," he said. "How's this? It registers nickels, dimes, and quarters."

"Oh!" Judy took the bank in her hand. It was small, but it had a professional look. "How much will it hold?" she asked.

"Ten dollars," Mr. Epstein said. "And when you get ten dollars, it opens and you can take out the money and put it in a savings bank. A regular one. Then you can start all over again." He turned the bank over and looked at the price tag. "It was two-fifty, but I'll let you have it for two dollars."

"Why that's lovely of you, Mr. Epstein. I have a bank, but I can shake the money out."

"That's no good."

140

"No, it isn't. Is it?" Judy said. She opened her bag and took out three dollars. "I'll take it."

"That'll be two fifty-five with tax. For the ledger and for the bank." He put his hand in his pocket and brought out forty-five cents change.

"Wait a minute," Judy said. She took two dollar bills from her bag and handed them to him. "May I have some change? You see, I plan to save two dollars and a half, and I'm going to put it right in the bank now."

He counted out two dollars in silver and gave the money to Judy. She set the bank down on the counter. "I'm going to drop in a nickel first," she said. She slipped five cents in the slot, and pulled a tiny lever to the right of the bank, and a bell tinkled faintly as the nickel dropped to the bottom. The dimes had a more silvery tone and the quarters were sensational. "Isn't it wonderful!" Judy exclaimed. "Isn't it wonderful!"

"It's a good bank," Mr. Epstein said. "A very good bank. You made a good buy."

Judy tucked the ledger under her arm and

picked up the bank. "Well, happy New Year," she said.

"Happy New Year!"

In her room once more, Judy set the bank on the corner of her desk and opened the ledger. On the top of the page she wrote the date, and above each column she printed "Debit" and "Credit." In the credit column she put, "Received from Mr. Harold Graves—$5.00," and in the debit column she wrote, "Cost of ledger —50 cents, tax—1 cent, cost of bank reduced from $2.50—$2.00, tax—4 cents." At the bottom of the page she wrote the totals: $5.00 on the credit side and $2.55 on the debit side. She looked at the bank, noting happily that it registered two dollars and forty-five cents, just five cents short of what she had planned to save. She reached for her pocketbook, and as she did so, the realization of what she had done struck her. Her stomach turned over and her hands grew cold. "Lois!" she called.

From across the hall, her mother's voice answered her. "Lois has gone out."

Judy got up from the desk and walked over to the window. She heard her mother come into the room, but she did not turn around.

"Well!" Mrs. Graves said. "What's this? A bank! And with two dollars and forty-five cents in it! That's splendid, darling! Just splendid! I think you are very wise to make such a sensible investment. To spend a little of your money for such a nice, practical bank and put your savings away *first*."

"Mom, where's Daddy?" Judy asked.

"He's gone to the club," Mrs. Graves said brightly. "To get a check cashed. He won't be long." She went over to Judy and kissed her lightly on the cheek. "He'll be proud of you, Judy."

Judy felt the veil on her mother's hat tickle the back of her neck. "Where are you going?" she asked dully.

"Just over to Madge's. When Daddy comes, tell him I'll be back about five." She patted Judy's shoulder and hurried from the room.

Judy heard the front door close, and she

walked back to the desk. She took the bank and put it in the side drawer of her desk. She closed the ledger and sat down, staring into space as a week of barren days moved by. There would be no lunches, no sodas or candy, no movies. Lois would see that she was not in the lunchroom and tell her mother, and the whole dreadful catastrophe would be exposed. Her allowance would be stopped and she would be put back on the old regime—enough money every day for that day's needs.

She sat quietly, her hands in her lap, in an agony of apprehension. She didn't hear her father when he came in until he called, "Anybody home?"

"I am," she answered. "Lois isn't, and Mom says to tell you she went to Madge's and that she'll be back about five."

She turned as her father entered the room. He smelled of the cold, of cigars, and of another, richer smell. He still wore his derby hat.

"Met Ted Kirby," he said. "What do you know about that? Haven't seen him in over ten

144

years. Hasn't changed a bit. I told him so, and he told me he'd have recognized me anywhere." He walked toward Judy and stood with his hand resting heavily on her shoulder. "How's the little capitalist?" he asked. "How is she?"

"Oh, I'm fine," Judy said. "I saved two dollars and forty-five cents."

She opened the drawer of her desk and brought out the bank.

"Well," he said. "Bought a bank, too?"

"Yes," Judy said. "And a ledger."

Mr. Graves picked up the bank and turned it over. He glanced hastily at the price tag, and again at the sum registered on the front of the bank. "It's a fine bank," he said. "Almost watertight." He didn't look at Judy, but pushed his hat back on his head and stared at the ceiling. "I tell you what," he said. "Just because you've saved so much out of your first allowance, I'll double it. Double the amount you've saved this week." He took out his wallet and gave her two dollar bills and then counted out forty-five cents in change.

"Oh!" Judy gasped. "Why, that's wonderful! It's just wonderful!"

"Well," Mr. Graves said grandly, "they say you can't take it with you." He began to whistle softly.

Judy, holding the money in her hand, suddenly felt as light as air.

9

Bury Me Not

NINE

Bury Me Not

Judy Graves had stood for a long time by the window looking down into the street. By pressing her face close to the glass, she could see the sidewalk near the curb and could see if a taxi drew up in front of the apartment house. Her breath clouded the windowpane, blurring the street lights, and she rubbed the glass clear with the palm of her hand. She could hear the sound of her sister Lois's pen as it scratched on the paper. When Lois wrote with a pen it was a sure sign she was using her best pink writing paper. Judy could hear the door to the kitchen swinging back and forth, and she could smell the tantalizing aroma of roast beef cooking in the kitchen.

She wished that Lois would finish her letter,

and she wanted to turn around to see if the letter was almost written, but she was afraid of missing the taxi when it stopped. "You'd better not use that blotter," she said.

"How can I concentrate when you're talking?" Lois asked. "It's bad enough to have you standing over there snuffling." She lifted her letter to make sure no ink had fallen on the desk blotter, and went on with her writing.

"Do you think Mom cried?" Judy said.

"Of course she didn't cry," Lois answered. "People don't cry just because they're at a funeral, not when they hardly knew the person that died."

"I never saw old Mrs. Wallace," Judy said. "Did you?"

"I saw her once."

Judy turned away from the window, pleasantly surprised. "Well, why didn't you say so?" she asked.

"I didn't consider it a matter of such vital importance," Lois said. She leaned back in the straight desk chair and shut her eyes, trying to bring back the picture of Mrs. Wallace. "She was sort of little and fat, and she was terribly old."

"Oh," Judy said. "I guess she didn't mind so much then. I mean it was *time*."

She turned back to the window and rested her forehead against the cold glass. The house seemed very quiet, and she hoped that when her father and mother came they would turn on the radio for the news, as they always did. She stretched out her tongue to see if she could touch the windowpane and made a small, moist dot. "I have never known anyone who died," she said. "Just animals."

"Well, don't keep talking about it," Lois told her. "*They* won't want to when they get home."

A taxi drew up in front of the building. "Here they are!" Judy exclaimed. Even down in the street, getting out of the cab, her mother and father looked different from other people, and she had known it was they the instant she saw

151

the top of her father's derby and the way her
mother stood as she waited near the edge of the
sidewalk.

"Here they come!" she called to Hilda in the
kitchen. "You can put dinner on, because
they're here!"

"You'd better not let Daddy see you using
his pen," she said to Lois.

Lois folded her letter and put it in a small
pink envelope. "I'm all through, anyway. And
I can't address it because I have to find out this
girl's number."

Judy went out to the hall and opened the
front door. She was standing there when her
father and mother got out of the elevator. "I
saw you paying the taximan, Daddy," she said.
"And I saw Mom fixing her hat."

Mr. and Mrs. Graves were silent. Mrs. Graves
stopped to kiss her, and Mr. Graves patted her
shoulder and went on into his bedroom.

"Don't hang on Mother when she's tired,"
Lois said. She took Mrs. Graves' coat and carried it to the hall closet.

Judy dropped her mother's arm. "Shall I turn on the radio?" she asked.

"No," Mrs. Graves answered. "Not tonight."

"Oh," Judy said. "Was it awful?"

Mrs. Graves took her handkerchief from her bag and Judy saw that it was crumpled and wet.

"Honestly, Judy!" Lois exclaimed.

Mr. Graves came into the living room and sat down in the big chair near the window. He wore a dark suit and a dark-blue tie with a small gray pin stripe. His face looked paler than usual, and his whole appearance seemed neater and more impersonal. "I'll tell you one thing, Grace," he said, "it's a terrible thing to go and not leave your house in order."

When he spoke, Judy had a picture of old Mrs. Wallace's house, the beds unmade, the ashtrays unemptied, and the dishes lying in the sink. "I thought she was rich," she said. "I thought she had a big house full of servants."

"Your father didn't mean what he said literally, Judy," Mrs. Graves told her. "He was speaking of loose ends." She sighed and turned

153

to her husband. "I know. I don't see why they thought of Beechwood. None of *her* people are there. They're all in Boston, and I feel that's what she would have wanted."

"Of course!" Mr. Graves exclaimed. "It's a lot of damned nonsense!"

"When I go," Mrs. Graves said, "I hope everyone will remember that I want to be buried in Manchester."

Judy went over and sat on the arm of her mother's chair. "Manchester," she repeated. "How pretty! Why, that's a lovely place to be buried in. I wouldn't mind being buried there. Unless I died at sea."

"A fat chance you have of dying at sea the way we go to Vermont summer after summer and never even see a sailboat," Lois said.

"I could be travelling," Judy said. "I could be torpedoed if the war keeps on."

"I don't like that Manchester one," Mr. Graves said. "It's neither one thing nor the other. It sits there in the middle of town, and

154

it's too flat. There's a dozen places that have a prettier view."

"Well, I hope they put me in that place down on Wall Street," Lois said. "I don't want to be stuck out in the country somewhere. I think it would be nice to be where there were a lot of people around."

Judy laughed scornfully. "You would! I think it's more romantic to be scattered to the wind."

Mr. Graves got up from his chair. "Would you like a spot of sherry before you eat?" he asked. He went to the kitchen and came back with four glasses and a bottle. Into two of the glasses he poured a thimbleful of sherry and handed them to Lois and Judy.

"This is nice," Mrs. Graves said, sipping her drink.

Mr. Graves held his glass to the light. "No, sir, no Manchester for me."

Judy took a drop of sherry on her tongue and tasted it appreciatively. "Well, where then, Daddy? Where?" she asked.

"Oh," Mr. Graves said, "I've had my spot picked out a long time. Do you remember the little place at Danby Four Corners?"

"Goodness!" Mrs. Graves exclaimed. "That jumping-off spot! Why, no one would ever be able to get up there. It's miles over the mountain on that rough road, and in the spring you couldn't even get a car through."

"Nevertheless," Mr. Graves said stubbornly, "that's the place for me. Right on top of a hill, plenty of light and air all around, and a view—well, you can't beat that view."

"Oh, it's lovely," Mrs. Graves admitted, "but you might just as well be in Timbuctoo."

"They don't put people in the place down on Wall Street any more, do they, Daddy?" Judy asked. "So that lets Lois out."

"You can't tell," Lois said. "By that time they might make an exception of me. For all you know, I may be famous, and they'd let me in just the way they would in Westminster Abbey."

"There're not ten families living in Danby

Four Corners," Mrs. Graves said. "And I'm sure I don't know what they do about keeping the place up."

"It does look sort of *poor*," Lois agreed.

Judy picked up her glass and carried it across the room and set it down on the small table by her father's chair. "Don't you think it's nice and exciting to be scattered to the winds, Daddy?" she asked.

"Not me."

"Well, now," Lois said. "Let's see. Mother wants to be in Manchester. Near the pond or on the side of the hill?"

"Near the pond," Mrs. Graves told her.

"All right. Mother's near the pond in Manchester," Lois went on. "Daddy's in Danby Four Corners."

"On the top of the hill," Mr. Graves said.

"On the top of the hill," Lois repeated. "I'm down in Wall Street in a vault, and Judy's scattered somewhere. Over the sea or over the land?"

"Over the sea, of course," Judy answered.

As she spoke, she could see her ashes blowing in the wind and floating gently down over the blue waves, lost and separated forever.

"How old was poor Mrs. Wallace, Mother?" she asked.

"Very old," Mrs. Graves told her. "Almost ninety."

"Ninety," Judy repeated. The room grew dim and the faces of her mother, father, and Lois became blurred. She seemed to be standing alone in an unfamiliar place. The place was too big and too dark, and she was small, and very old. She was ninety, and she was the only one left.

She took a quick step backward and felt her father's hand. "Here," he said. "Your mother spoke to you. Have you washed your hands for dinner?"

10

Appreciation of Art

TEN

Appreciation of Art

THE auditorium of the Carlton School was crowded and noisy. The children from the lower grades had marched in and were seated in the front rows, where they twisted and uttered unintelligible, piercing cries. Occasionally Miss Moffatt, who taught American history, walked down the aisle and frowned at them, putting her finger to her lips. For a few minutes they would be still. Then they would begin to move and rustle again, and pull and shove at one another.

The performance of "The Tempest" given by the girls of the Junior School was scheduled to begin at eight-thirty, and at a quarter past eight almost every seat was filled. Lois Graves, who was usher in Aisle 3, had put her coat

161

across two of the best seats in the twelfth row, so that when her parents arrived, fashionably late, she was ready for the emergency. She met them at the door and smiled at them politely. She wore a powder-blue taffeta evening dress that swept the floor, and stretched diagonally over one shoulder was a dark-green satin ribbon on which the word "Usher" was printed in large gold letters. In one hand she carried a flashlight and in the other she held some programs.

"Well, dear," Mrs. Graves said. She looked quickly at the other ushers to see if Lois's dress was quite suitable, and sighed with relief as she noted other taffeta dresses in pink, turquoise blue, and pale green. She noticed that little Mildred Farney's dress pulled too tightly across her breasts, and that Jane Turner had on an unbecoming shade of blue. "Well, dear," she repeated.

Lois turned away, brisk and professional, and led the way down the aisle. She walked neatly in her high heels, and when she reached the seats over which she had thrown her coat, she pressed the button of her flashlight and focussed the beam on the floor.

"Say," Mr. Graves said appreciatively, "this is great!"

Lois leaned over them. "You'd better hold my coat so that people won't—you know."

The woman in the adjoining seat stared at them and muttered, "Well, I *must* say!"

"Oh," Mrs. Graves said. "Do you think you should have, Lois?"

"Nuts," Lois whispered. "Don't pay any attention to that old gorilla. She's just mad because she wanted to sit on the aisle and I told her these seats were taken."

With a whirl of her skirts and a rustle of silk, she was gone.

Mrs. Graves put her hand on her husband's sleeve. "It was thoughtful of her just the same."

Mr. Graves opened his program and fished in his pocket for his glasses. "I don't believe I've ever seen 'The Tempest.' What's it about?"

"I'm sure I don't know," Mrs. Graves answered. "I've never even read it. Judy's playing Stephano. It's a boy's part." She held her program two feet away from her eyes and frowned. "Here it is. Here's her name. Judith Graves."

Mr. Graves adjusted his glasses. "Stephano, a drunken Butler," he read aloud.

"Well!" Mrs. Graves exclaimed. "Well!"

A sharp memory of a talk he had had with Judy a week before flashed into Mr. Graves' mind. "Daddy," she had asked, "how many drinks do you have to have before you get drunk?" And he had answered, "It all depends. A person might get drunk on one drink, and then again it might take twenty." "I suppose," Judy had persisted, "if you were used to it, it would take twenty." He had said he imagined it would. And Judy seemed satisfied.

Mrs. Graves looked at him anxiously. "I suppose they know what they're doing. Giving a part like that to a little girl, I mean."

"Oh, sure," he said.

She glanced at her program thoughtfully. "I

164

think it would have been nice if they had decided to give 'The Mikado.' They planned to at first. Except there weren't enough girls who could sing. Here's Fuffy Adams' name. She's going to be Trinculo, a Jester."

"I saw Pete Adams when we came in. He's putting on weight."

"They rented the costumes. Even the wigs."

"Have you seen Judy's costume?" Mr. Graves asked.

"No," she answered. "They only got them yesterday, in time for dress rehearsal. I haven't even heard her lines. She said them for Hilda, but it was the night we played bridge with the Conovers. I heard her in the kitchen, though, and she seemed to be shouting."

"I wouldn't worry."

"Oh, I'm not worrying. After all, Miss Lucy Smith is coaching them, and she must know what she's doing."

There were signs of excitement among the children in the first rows, and at a signal from a slender, faded, blonde woman who appeared from a door at the left, fifteen of them arose and marched up the stairs onto the stage. They stood there swallowing nervously, their arms hanging limply at their sides. Their dresses had become mussed and their eyes were glassy. The blonde woman, a Miss Avery, sat down at the piano and struck an opening chord.

"It's the school song," Mrs. Graves whispered. "I suppose we ought to stand."

According to the program, the words to the school song had been written by a Miss Dorothy Brewer, '09, but the tune was "Flow Gently, Sweet Afton."

Mrs. Graves watched the young faces of the Junior Glee Club tenderly, and her heart melted within her. They started to sing slightly off key, but the sound of their own voices gave them reassurance, and the words rang out clear and sweet:

The mem'ries of school days will never grow old, So raise high the colors, the green and the gold.

For no reason at all, her eyes smarted, and she fumbled in her evening bag for a handkerchief.

Our dear Alma Mater, our own Carlton School, May she evermore flourish and over us rule.

As the song ended there was a burst of applause, which stopped abruptly as Miss Avery swung into the opening bars of "The Star-Spangled Banner." The audience joined enthusiastically in the singing.

"I imagine the play will begin now," Mrs. Graves said, rearranging her evening wrap on the back of the seat. "I wonder when Judy comes on. It would be funny if we didn't recognize her, wouldn't it?"

"We'll know her, all right," Mr. Graves said.

The girls of the Junior Glee Club marched back to their places and the lights grew dim. The curtains parted, showing a black backdrop. There was a flash of lightning from above and the sound of tinny thunder. The play had begun.

"They've got the stage awfully dark," Mrs. Graves whispered. "Can you see Judy?"

"I think this crowd are supposed to be sailors. They look as though they're pulling at ropes."

The voices of the girls were lost in the rolls of thunder, and the curtain fell.

"Well, that was short, anyway," Mr. Graves said. "The next scene is on an island."

The curtain rose again; the backdrop had been lifted and the stage was larger. In the direct centre at the rear was an opening surrounded by unbleached muslin that had been dyed gray with green spots to represent a rocky entrance to a cave, and to the right of this stood a small spruce tree in a tub. From the wings came two figures, both strictly feminine, although one of them wore a long, gray, matted beard, a shaggy white wig, black tights, and a doublet. "Prospero," Mrs. Graves said. "And that's Miranda with him. The Burchell child."

Miranda had on a black wig bound with a fillet. It was made of the blackest hair Mrs. Graves had ever seen, and from under it Polly

Burchell's face peered, small and round. She walked with the slow, forlorn gait of an over-worked chambermaid in a second-rate hotel, but as she began to speak she came to life and gestured with her arms. When she finished her lines, she lapsed into a coma and stared out into the audience during the time Prospero took up the plot. The scene was long, and Mrs. Graves was glad when Ariel danced from the wings. Ariel's tunic was embarrassingly short, and she seemed to be suffering from an acute form of St. Vitus's dance.

"What's the matter with her?" Mr. Graves asked.

"I imagine Miss Smith told her to keep moving, the poor little thing. She's supposed to be a sprite, you see."

The play dragged on. As each character appeared for the first time, there was a burst of applause from relatives and school friends. Mrs. Graves sat tensely, waiting for Judy's entrance. But Act I ended and there had been no sign of her.

"She probably has just a small part," Mrs. Graves said when the lights went up. "The girls *do* mutter, don't they?" She clapped halfheartedly. "I don't see how Judy can be a *drunken* butler. After all, it's supposed to be an almost deserted island, and there couldn't very well be any liquor on it. At least, I don't see where it would come from. The ship is wrecked. Besides, I don't think Judy would know how to act drunk. As far as I know, she's never even seen anyone very drunk."

"Of course she hasn't," Mr. Graves said. "A little high, maybe, but not boiled."

They waited for her entrance until Act II, Scene 2. A small, fat Caliban, dressed in what looked to be a fur union suit, and Fuffy Adams as Trinculo were talking together when Mrs. Graves heard a voice singing in the wings. It was the first completely audible voice in the performance, and it was Judy's. She reeled onto the stage, a bottle in her hand. Her smooth, dark-brown hair was covered with a straw-colored wig, the tip of her nose was painted a bright red. Her clothes were awry and she looked as tight as an owl.

"This is a very scurvy tune to sing at a man's funeral. Well, here's my comfort," she shouted, and, lifting the bottle to her lips, she took a healthy swig.

The children in the audience broke into delighted laughter, and Judy, hearing them, lifted the bottle again and staggered across the stage, throwing a heavy arm around Fuffy Adams, who giggled with abandon.

The force of Judy's entrance took Caliban off guard and struck her dumb. She forgot her rôle of savage and deformed slave and stood by as quietly as a baby panda in her furry suit, watching Judy's antics. Each time Judy lifted the bottle to her lips the laughter from the lower grades got louder. Over the noise, Judy's voice rang out, blurred with drink, loud and insinuating. She spun around, crying, "Prithee, do not turn me about. My stomach is not constant." And as an added touch, she put her hand on her small, firm stomach and hiccoughed.

171

When the curtain fell, the applause was deafening. It continued until Judy stood alone on the stage. She lifted the bottle to her lips and reeled again.

Mr. and Mrs. Graves were silent as the lights went on. Finally, Mrs. Graves spoke. "I can't believe it. I can't imagine what's got into her." She looked at her husband and saw that he was smiling.

"You could hear her, anyway," he said.

"Oh, you could hear her, all right."

They sat through the next three acts and watched Judy faithfully portray various stages of intoxication; she fought, she laughed senselessly, she was sad, she lapsed into self-pity, and her last line, spoken in a maudlin whine—"O! touch me not. I am not Stephano, but a cramp" —brought down the house.

She gave a superb performance. She took four curtain calls and her cheeks were flushed and her eyes bright. The flowers that Mr. Graves had sent were delivered over the footlights, and she stood holding them in one hand while she clutched the bottle with the other.

Mrs. Graves slipped her wrap over her shoulders. "I wonder where Lois is. I hope she isn't minding too much."

"Judy was good," Mr. Graves said. "She was damned good."

They walked up the aisle. At the door, Pete Adams stopped them and clapped Mr. Graves on the shoulders. "Best thing I ever saw, the act your daughter put on!" he cried. "Reminded me of you, Harry." He wiped the tears from his eyes and coughed convulsively. "Congratulations, Grace! Congratulations!"

Mrs. Graves caught sight of Miss Lucy Smith and glanced hastily away. But Miss Smith bore down on them. She was a plump, white-haired woman, and she was smiling. "Wasn't Judy marvellous?" she said. "I had no idea she had it in her. She didn't act at all like that at rehearsals. To tell you the truth"—she lowered her voice —"I thought she made the other girls seem a trifle *wooden*."

The door to the basement opened and the members of the cast streamed out. In the centre of the group was Judy. She had taken off her wig and her soft hair fell to her shoulders. She carried the property bottle in one hand and her face was streaked with makeup. In her eyes shone a look of utter joy and pride. With her, holding tightly to her arm, was Lois, who caught sight of her father and mother. "Here she is!" she called. "Here's Judy! Talk about your Moscow Art Theatre for real swell acting!"

Judy ran toward them and Mrs. Graves caught her in her arms. She smelled of grease paint, perspiration, and moth balls, and she was trembling.

For an instant she buried her face against her mother, and Mrs. Graves knew that she was close to tears. "You were lovely, Judy darling," she whispered.

"You were great!" Mr. Graves said, and patted her head roughly.

Children crowded around them and teachers and parents stopped to congratulate them. Judy seemed to be living in a dream. She leaned closer to her mother and then shook herself free. "Here," she said, and handed the bottle to her father. "Miss Smith says I can keep this for a souvenir. Hold it for me, will you, while I change my clothes?"

Mr. Graves took the bottle, which was made of papier-mâché, and tucked it proudly under his arm. "You run along," he said. "We'll wait here for you. And take your time. There's no hurry."

11

Les Temps Perdus

ELEVEN

Les Temps Perdus

Mr. Graves was sitting in the large chair by the window, a pencil in his hand and the magazine section of the Sunday *Herald Tribune*, opened at the crossword-puzzle page, lying across his knees, when his daughter Judy came into the room. She carried a pad of paper under her arm and had tucked a pencil behind one ear. Mr. Graves hastily picked up the magazine section and studied it, frowning intently. For a moment there was no sound in the room except the soft beat of the rain against the windowpanes and a slight rustle of paper as Judy switched the pad from one arm to the other. Finally Mr. Graves looked toward her. She was staring at him fixedly, and he saw that her hair was mussed and that her forehead was moist and shiny with perspiration. Her appearance, combined with the steam on the inside of the windows and the dripping rain outside, made him feel that the whole room had a sticky, unpleasant atmosphere.

Seeing that she had his attention, she walked toward him and sat down on the broad window sill. "Daddy, do you mind answering a few things?" she asked.

"What sort of things?"

"Oh, nothing like arithmetic," she said. "Just some things about yourself and Mom, like where you were born and stuff."

"I was born in Brooklyn," Mr. Graves said. "And your mother was born in Kansas City, Missouri. You're not sending away for something, or anything like that, are you?"

"There's a girl in our class whose father was born in New Zealand," Judy said. "She's quite an interesting girl. Her grandfather was sort of a pioneer."

Mr. Graves laughed shortly. "If I remember

180

correctly, a great many people who went to New Zealand and Australia were sent there because they were criminals. You can call that interesting if you like."

"*I* think it's interesting," Judy said calmly. She leaned back against the window and put her feet up on the arm of his chair.

"You'd better not let your mother catch you doing that," Mr. Graves warned her.

"Her door's locked. I rattled the knob and she didn't say anything, so I think she must be asleep."

Judy took the pencil from behind her ear and wrote on the pad, "Father's birthplace—Brooklyn. Mother's birthplace—Kansas City, Missoura." "I'm writing my autobiography," she explained. "I *have* to. Everybody in our class has to."

"Well, say," Mr. Graves said, sitting up straighter, "that isn't such a bad idea. What do you want to know?"

"Just outstanding events," she said. "If I put

181

in every little thing, it will be too long. I've thought of loads about myself, but I wanted you and Mom for a sort of background."

Mr. Graves looked out the window thoughtfully. "Well," he said, "I was born in Brooklyn and went to public school there until I went to Kent. Then, when I got through Kent, I went to Yale, and a few years after the war I married your mother."

Judy wrote hastily on the pad. "Yes?" she asked.

"Well, that's about all."

"You were in the war, weren't you?"

"I was and I wasn't," Mr. Graves said. "I was in the Army, second lieutenant, but I never got over."

Judy sighed. "That isn't very much, is it?"

"It was all that I could handle at the time," Mr. Graves said.

"It isn't much, just the same," Judy said. "What did Grandpa do?"

"He was in the insurance business," Mr. Graves answered. "He was born in Brooklyn, too. And *his* father came from up near Binghamton, New York. My mother was born in New Haven and, as far as I know, all her folks came from there. They were all connected with the New York, New Haven & Hartford Railroad."

Judy sighed again, deeply. "And I was born in New York," she said. "And so was Lois. Did you *ever*!"

"What's wrong with being born in New York?" Mr. Graves asked.

"Oh, I don't know," Judy said. "It just seems sort of funny, that's all. What about Mom?"

"Well, as I told you, she was born in Kansas City, Missouri, and her father was vice-president of some wholesale dry-goods store there. I think his father came from Pennsylvania originally, but you'd better ask her."

"I wonder why he stayed in Kansas City?" Judy asked. "I wonder why he didn't push on farther West."

"He had a darned good business," Mr. Graves said. "A darned good business. Your mother's father, I mean. He had six children and he managed to send them all to college. Why, I met your mother when she was a junior at Smith."

There was the sound of a key turning in a lock in one of the doors that opened into the hall, and Mrs. Graves, dressed in a turquoise-blue house coat, came into the living room. "I must have fallen asleep," she said, brightly. "What are you two up to?"

"Judy has to write her autobiography for school," Mr. Graves explained, "and I'm giving her some facts."

"Not about Uncle Will, I hope," Mrs. Graves said.

Judy looked at her sharply. "What about Uncle Will?" she asked. "Whose Uncle Will?"

"Your father's uncle."

"What about him?"

"Oh, nothing," Mrs. Graves said. "I was just joking, really. He was a very *sweet* person. Just unfortunate. I, personally, was very fond of him, and we mustn't speak ill of the dead."

"Oh, of course not," Judy said, soberly. "Would you like to hear what I've written so far? It's mostly about myself and Lois. I was going to put you in later, when I copied it."

Mrs. Graves sat down on the couch and rubbed her eyes. "Maybe Lois would like to hear it, too. Where is she?"

"She's in the bathroom steaming her face," Judy said. "She took a whole tray of ice cubes, and when she's through steaming, she's going to rub ice on it to tighten her muscles and keep them from sagging."

"Lois!" Mrs. Graves called. "Come right out of that bathroom and leave your face alone. Remember what happened when you used the pore cream."

Mr. and Mrs. Graves and Judy sat silently until Lois came slowly into the room. Her face was red and blotched, and her light, soft hair was held back from her forehead by a circular comb.

"Look at you!" her mother said.

185

"It's just the circulation being stimulated that did it," Lois said. "It'll go away. It *feels* wonderful. What do you want?"

"Judy's written part of her autobiography that she has to do for school. I thought you'd like to hear it."

Lois sat down on the arm of her father's chair. "I'll say," she said.

"Well," Judy said. "Shall I begin?" She took two sheets of folded paper out from under her sweater and opened them. "It hasn't any title."

"You can think of one later," Mrs. Graves said. "Go ahead."

Judy cleared her throat and began to read. "It was exactly on the stroke of midnight on the twenty-first of September that I was born."

"Judy!" Mrs. Graves said. "How did you get it into your head that you were born on the stroke of midnight? You were born at eight in the morning."

"A few minutes after eight. Almost ten past, I think it was," Mr. Graves said. "I remember I got to the office about nine-thirty."

"It isn't so very important," Judy said.

"In an autobiography," Mrs. Graves told her, "one should be accurate."

"I'll fix it," Judy said, and went on with her reading. "It was a wild stormy night and our old family doctor fought his way through the terrible rain to reach the bedside of my mother who hovered between life and death." She looked up. "I sort of got that idea from 'David Copperfield,'" she explained. "But I can change that, too."

"I should think so!" Mrs. Graves said. "I think you'd better cut that whole part out altogether. You were born in a very nice little private hospital on Central Park West. It's been torn down now."

"Well, anyway," Judy said, and started to read again. "I was a small fat healthy baby, and from the first objected to being called 'the image' of any other member of the family because I knew I was different."

Lois gave a short, coarse laugh. "The other members of the family were the ones who objected," she said.

"That will do, Lois," Mr. Graves said. "Go on, Judy."

"At that time," Judy continued, "my mother and father were a very affectionate couple and he called her Pidge which was short for Pigeon."

"Listen—" Mr. Graves said.

"Just a minute, Harry," Mrs. Graves interrupted. "What Dad was going to say, I'm sure, was that such things are sort of—well, sort of family jokes. And I'm sure your teacher doesn't want you to write about them. I think she wants you to tell all about where you went to school and what you did there. Things like those."

Judy made a cryptic sign on the edge of the paper with her pencil. "My sister Lois was born two years before I was, shortly after Mom and Dad were married. As a nickname Dad and Mom called her T. P. for Third Person and this later changed to Tippet. So as Tippet at home and Lois at school she was known for a number of years."

"Tippet!" Lois repeated. "I haven't been called Tippet for years, Judy Graves, and you know it! I haven't been called Tippet once since I've been going to the Carleton School, and I'm not going to have you noising it around all over the place. She simply can't put that in. Can she, Mother?"

"Well," Mrs. Graves said doubtfully, "you *were* called Tippet. I think it's a rather sweet little nickname. Why can't Judy simply say that your nickname was Tippet and not explain *how* you happened to be called that?"

"She can't," Lois said. "She simply can't. Or I'll fix her."

"Well, do you want to hear the rest of this or don't you?" Judy asked. She cleared her throat again. "When I was seven I was forced to attend a public school for four months. It was in 1933 when my father who is in Wall Street had suffered heavy losses and couldn't pay for a private school. The public school was terrible! I was the only nice child in the class and for those four months was teacher's pet."

Mr. Graves got up from his chair and walked toward the fireplace, where he stood with his hands in his pockets, looking helplessly at Mrs. Graves.

"Do you know, Judy," Mrs. Graves said, "I hardly think *that* part is fair to Dad. After all, it was only for four months, and the school wasn't bad. Not bad at all. *Not* that I want you to think for a minute that I regret sending you there. But it just isn't fair to Dad. After all, it was the only time you *ever* went to public school, and it was for such a short time. Besides, it isn't considered very nice for little girls to talk about money. Don't you remember how I've told you *never* to ask what things cost? Well, what I mean is, this is the same sort of thing."

"It was a terrible school," Judy said.

"Well," Mrs. Graves said cheerily, "it's all over and done with now, so don't you think it would be better if you just *forgot* it?"

"Nineteen-thirty-three," Mr. Graves said. "God!"

"Yes, Harry," his wife murmured, "I know." She went over to Judy and sat down beside her on the window sill.

"Now, let's see," she said. "Let's see if we can't think of something interesting that happened in our family a long time ago. Something about Grandma or Grandpa, perhaps. Something that will make a nice, interesting story for your teacher to read."

"There isn't anything," Judy said. "I asked Dad."

Lois fidgeted uneasily on the arm of the chair, and Mr. Graves stood quietly by the fireplace, a peculiar look in his eyes. Mrs. Graves frowned. "Now, let's see." She turned her head to look out at the driving rain. In the back of her mind an idea stirred and she remembered snatches of a story that someone had told her or that she had read.

"I have it!" she exclaimed. "It seems to me that my mother told me once that her great-grandfather was a pirate!"

"A pirate!" Judy repeated.

"Yes, a pirate! And I think I can think of a story or two about him. He lived in a very lonely part of England and once he cut off the

191

ears of a bandit who was terrorizing the countryside. Cut them off with his sword."

"Cut off his *ears*?"

"Cut them right off. And when he first came to this country, he was a very young man. And one day he saw the Governor's daughter and fell in love with her. It was in Virginia, I think. Anyway, you can make it Virginia. Well, he went right to the Governor and asked for his daughter's hand, and the Governor refused, so do you know what he did?"

"No," Judy said.

"He waited until the Governor's daughter was being married to another man, and he went to the wedding, and right in the middle of the ceremony he swore in loud tones that could be heard all over the church that he would marry the lady's daughter if she had one. And she did have one, and he did!"

"Golly!" Judy exclaimed. "That's wonderful. Dad didn't tell me anything like that."

"I don't think I ever told Daddy about it," Mrs. Graves said.

"It's swell," Judy said. "*Really* swell."

The autobiography that she had written slipped from her lap and fell to the floor unnoticed.

"And if you like," Mrs. Graves went on, "I'll sit right here with you and help you with it."

"I know what I can call it," Judy said. "I can call it 'I'm Partially Pirate.'"

Mrs. Graves, looking down, saw that Judy's stubby brown oxfords were resting on the pale-beige slipcover of the chair. She opened her mouth to say something, and almost immediately closed it again.

"'I'm Partially Pirate,'" Judy repeated, her eyes shining. "Don't you think that'll be better?"

"Yes," Mrs. Graves answered. "Much better!"

12

Primrose Path

TWELVE

Primrose Path

Judy Graves opened the pale-blue envelope addressed to her in Mary Caswell's handwriting. She was prepared for the invitation it contained, but she was not prepared for the formal and elegant wording. To the left of the page, on the upper corner, was a butterfly printed in a darker shade of blue, and underneath it was Mary's name, also printed. The invitation, which was written in longhand, read:

Miss Mary Caswell
Requests the pleasure of
Miss Judy Graves' company
At a dance to be given at her home,
Twenty East Seventy-eighth Street,
New York City,
on
Friday, February Twenty-first,
Nineteen Hundred and Forty-One.
R.S.V.P.

Judy stared at it, impressed. "Well," she said. "What do you know about that!"

Her sister, Lois, who was rubbing vaseline into her eyebrows in front of the dressing-table mirror, turned around. "What is it?" she asked.

"It's the invite to Mary's dance," Judy said. "And it's formal."

Lois took the sheet of paper. "How too silly! If she was trying to be ritzy, why didn't she have them engraved? And a dance for a lot of kids. You'll trample one another to death. Thank heavens, I don't have to go."

"You're too old," Judy said. "I wonder if Mrs. Caswell will stay in her room the whole time the way Mrs. Adams did when Fuffy had her party."

"Well, if she does, there won't be much dancing," Lois said. "The boys will go into a huddle and the whole thing will end in a brawl. Besides, what are you going to dance *to*? Victrola records or the radio or something?"

"To records," Judy told her. "Mary wanted a band, but there wasn't room. Mr. Caswell is going to change the records. They're going to move the victrola out into the hall so he won't be in the way."

She took the invitation from Lois and read it again. "I don't get it," she said. "Mrs. Caswell wrote one out for a sample and Mary brought it to school. It wasn't like this one at all. It just said that Mary was going to have a party. Jean Drummond told Mary it was too babyish, and she loaned Mary an etiquette book. I guess Mary copied this one out of the book."

"I wouldn't know."

"Well," Judy said, "I better get going. I have to be at Fuffy's this morning to meet a friend of her brother's. If it's all right, he's going to take me to the dance."

"If what's all right?" Lois asked.

"Oh, you know." Judy's eyelids fluttered nervously. "If it's O.K. If he says he won't, Mrs. Adams told Barlow he'd have to take both Fuffy and me."

Lois's laugh was scornful. "Before I'd go and be looked over like a prize horse or something!"

"I don't mind," Judy said mildly. She went to

her closet and took out her coat and hat. "Barlow says he doesn't like girls."

"Who?"

"This boy. His name is Haskell Cummings. He's going to Exeter next year." Judy smoothed her hair carefully before she put on her hat. "Barlow says he really doesn't mind girls so much if they're good sports. Well, I'll be seeing you."

"Mmm," Lois murmured. She turned back to the mirror and again massaged her eyebrows gently.

When Judy rang the bell at the Adamses' apartment, Fuffy opened the door. "They're in Barlow's room," she whispered. "They're throwing darts."

"Oh," Judy said. She followed Fuffy into the living room and took off her coat and hat and laid them across the arm of the couch. "How tall is he?" she asked.

"As tall as you are. Maybe a little bit taller," Fuffy said. "If they don't come out pretty soon, I'll call them."

200

"You'd better not," Judy said. "They'll have to come out sometime."

Fuffy sat down on the couch. "Maybe you're right," she said. "Mom asked them if they didn't want to stay for lunch with us, but they said they'd rather eat at the Automat."

"The Automat *is* nice."

The two girls were silent. They could hear the sound of the darts as they hit the target, which was nailed to the door of Barlow's room, and they could hear Barlow's voice as he called "Bull's-eye!"

"Let's play cards or something," Judy said. "It will look funny if they find us just sitting here waiting."

"O.K.," Fuffy said. She went to the hall closet and got out the card table. "Beat you at double Canfield!" Her voice was loud and enthusiastic. She set the table up and, taking two packs of cards from the desk drawer, held them out to Judy. "Which'll you have? The reds or the greens?"

"The reds." Judy drew a straight chair up to

the table and began to shuffle. "Have you answered your invitation yet?"

"What did you think of it?" Fuffy asked. "Did you ever?"

"Well," Judy said, "I suppose she wanted it formal."

"Formal!" Fuffy laughed. "I thought it looked lousy."

"It did look funny," Judy agreed. "But that's on account of Mary's handwriting. I think it was all right, though. I mean the way it was put."

"It slayed Daddy. And Mom says she doesn't think Mrs. Caswell *knew*. She thinks Mary did it on her own."

"Oh, I don't doubt *that*," Judy said. "I don't doubt that at all." She put a two and a three of hearts on Fuffy's ace.

The door of Barlow's room opened, and at the sound the two girls began to laugh shrilly. "Oh!" Fuffy screamed. "You rat! That was my ace!"

They started to play furiously, slapping the cards down on the table and knocking them to the floor in their excitement. They appeared to be too engrossed in their game to look up as the boys entered the room.

"And a nine, and a ten, and a jack!" Judy cried. "I can't move until you get something. Get a hump on! You're too slow!"

Fuffy went through the remaining cards in her hand once more. "I'm bust, too," she said. She glanced at the boys carelessly. "Hello. Oh, that's right, Haskell. You don't know Judy Graves, do you? Judy, this is Haskell Cummings."

Judy stopped sorting the cards long enough to look up and smile. "Hello," she said. "Hello, Barlow."

The two boys moved nearer the table, and Fuffy counted the score. "Thirty-nine for you, Judy. And only *twenty* for me!"

Judy threw herself back heavily in the chair. "Wow! I'm bushed!" she said. "Well, I'm nineteen ahead anyway. Of course, it doesn't matter as long as we're not playing for money."

Haskell Cummings took a dime from his

pocket, tossed it into the air, and caught it expertly. "I took this away from Adams," he said.

The girls looked at him in admiration. He was a slender boy with straight, light hair that fell over his forehead. He wore a belted tweed jacket and long, pale-gray trousers. His nose was slightly hooked and his chin receded only slightly, thanks to the family dentist, who had been working on it for five years.

"I wish," Fuffy said, "that Mary would have games. Not silly games, you know, but real ones with cards."

"Me too," Judy said. "I've known how to play poker for years."

"Even if she doesn't," Fuffy went on, "there's no good reason why we four can't play something if we want to. After all, what's the good of *dancing* all evening?"

"Well, I said I'd go, but I didn't say I'd dance." Barlow kicked at the leg of the bridge table.

"I tell you what we could do," Judy said. "We could do exactly what we *want*. I mean what's

204

the sense of sitting around like sticks? As long as we *have* to go, we might as well have some fun. We had loads of fun at your party, Fuffy."

"What happened?" Haskell Cummings asked.

"Oh, that's right, you weren't there," Judy said. "It was last year and I guess you didn't know Barlow then. Well, for one thing, we threw water out the window."

"Judy hit a man on the street." Fuffy laughed and shook her head at the happy memory. "For a while we thought he was going to come up and complain or something. But he didn't. Not that we'd of cared."

"If he had come," Judy said, "I'd of told him to go sell his papers."

"Judy's *crazy*," Fuffy said loyally. "She'll do anything.

Haskell Cummings looked at Judy speculatively, and she stared back at him unflinching. "I'll do anything when I happen to feel like it," she said.

"She's the best basketball player at school," Fuffy said.

"Oh, for heaven's sake!" Judy protested modestly.

"Where do you go in the summer?" Haskell Cummings asked her.

"South Dorset, Vermont," Judy said. "We've been going there for years. Where do you go?"

"Madison, Connecticut," he answered.

"I've been there. I visited my Aunt Julia there one summer."

"Do you know Jane Garside?" Haskell Cummings asked.

Judy held her breath and took the plunge. "That drip," she said.

Haskell's face lighted up. "Drip is right!" he said. "Where did you swim? At the Yacht Club or at the Country Club?"

"At the Country Club," Judy answered. She waited for Haskell Cummings' decision.

"That's where I swim," he said.

"Well, isn't that the funniest thing!" Judy said, and began to laugh. There was relief and excitement in her laughter.

"Hey, look out!" Fuffy warned her. "You'll get the hiccoughs!"

"Oh, don't!" Judy gasped. "Every time you say that, I *do* get them. And"—she drew in her breath—"I *have* got them!"

"Grab her arms! Grab her arms, and hold them over her head, and I'll get the vinegar!" Fuffy cried, and ran to the kitchen.

Haskell Cummings sprang into action and, taking Judy's arms, he yanked them in the air. "Somebody scare her!" he called. He let her arms go and, grabbing the back of her chair, tipped it over until it almost reached the floor. She shrieked wildly as he tilted the chair down and brought it swiftly up again. Her hair fell over her face and she giggled weakly.

"Well," Fuffy asked, as she came back into the room carrying the vinegar bottle, "how are they?"

Judy waited, scarcely breathing. "They're gone," she said. "Haskell cured them."

"That's the first time I've ever known Judy to have the hiccoughs and get over them like that," Fuffy said.

"When they get hiccoughs, the best thing to do is to scare them," Haskell said.

"It certainly worked, all right," Judy said. "Thanks a lot."

"Well," Barlow said, "we'd better get going."

"Thanks an *awful* lot," Judy said.

Haskell pulled down his tweed jacket and straightened his tie. "I can almost always cure hiccoughs," he said.

The two boys went out in the hall to get their hats and coats, and Fuffy followed them. Judy could hear them as they whispered together. Fuffy came back into the room as the front door closed.

"It's all right," she said. "He's going to take you. He says you are a darned good sport and not a *bit* affected."

They looked at one another and smiled. "I think he's nice," Judy said. "And we can have some fun now. I mean, we can stir up something and not poke around dancing."

"Oh, dancing!" Fuffy said. "Phooey to that stuff."

In the week that followed, Judy called Fuffy up every night to talk about the party, and by the time Friday arrived she was weak with excitement. She bathed before dinner, which was served at half past six on her account. And when she had finished her dessert, Mrs. Graves offered to help her get into her dress.

"No, thanks just the same," Judy said. "Just keep Lois out of the way. She makes me nervous picking on me."

"Well, don't yank at your dress too hard when you pull it down or the net will tear," her mother said.

Judy laughed. "It'll probably be a *wreck* before the night's over! Fuffy and Haskell and Barlow and I aren't going to bother much about *dancing. We're* going to play games and stuff."

"Don't be too rough," Mrs. Graves said.

The lamp on the bureau was lighted when Judy went into the room she shared with Lois. She closed the door and took off her flannel bathrobe, standing in front of her mirror in a white slip that reached to the floor. Earlier in the day she had rolled up the ends of her hair in curlers, and now she began to unfasten them slowly. Her dark-brown hair, which usually fell straight to her shoulders, lay in soft curls around her head. She fluffed it out and, going to the closet, took out her new white net dress. Although she had bought it early in January with the money her Aunt Julia had sent her for Christmas, there had been no occasion to wear it before. It had a long, full skirt, caught up in places by tiny blue bows, and there was another, larger bow on the right shoulder. She slipped it over her head. As she walked back to the mirror, the skirt swirled and rustled about her feet.

Leaning closer to the mirror, she rested her elbows on the top of the bureau, her chin in the palms of her hands. The light from the lamp cast oblique shadows across her face. Her eyes looked bright and dark, and her hair was a dusky contrast against the whiteness of her throat. She tilted her head up, lowered her eyes, and studied herself through her lashes. The round fullness of her face seemed to fade, and she could see the outlines of her cheekbones.

She looked older and slimmer. "I look as pretty as Lois," she thought.

For a long while she stood there, her eyes half closed. Then she turned and, walking briskly across the room, opened the top bureau drawer of Lois's bureau. She found a small bottle of pale-pink nail polish and, sitting on the edge of the bed, she carefully applied it to her nails. When the polish was dry, she put the bottle back in the drawer and rummaged around until she found a small white enamel compact and a rose-colored Roger & Gallet lipstick. She brushed the powder on her face and neck and applied the lipstick. In her own handkerchief case she found a large white chiffon handkerchief embroidered with pink roses, and she carefully wrapped the compact and lipstick in it.

Once more she leaned close to the mirror, and fell in love with what she saw reflected there. Her blue satin slippers were soft on her feet, and her dress, billowing out below the waist, gave her a sense of lightness and well-

211

being. She heard the doorbell ring and knew that Haskell Cummings had arrived to take her to the dance.

There was a rap on the door, and her mother's voice called "Judy!"

"In a minute," she answered.

She picked up the handkerchief, opened the door, and walked across the hall to the living room. Haskell Cummings was talking to her mother and father and Lois. He stood with his back to Judy as she entered the room. He wore a dark-blue suit and his hair was brushed slickly back.

Mr. Graves looked up at Judy. "Well," he said. "Well."

Haskell Cummings turned around. He started to say "Hiyah there, Judy," but the words died in his throat.

"Good evening," Judy said, and held out her hand. "Aren't you nice to be so prompt!"

Something about the tone of her voice made him feel that he had been more than prompt, that he had been too early.

"We don't have to go yet if you don't want to," he said. "We can wait a while."

"Oh, goodness, it doesn't matter. As long as you're here we might as well go," Judy said.

Mr. Graves got up from his chair. "I'll get your cape," he said. He went to the hall closet and brought Judy's cape to her.

"Here, Haskell," she said, handing him the compact and lipstick wrapped in her chiffon handkerchief. "Keep these in your pocket for me. I'm simply terrible. I lose everything."

He tucked them into the pocket of his coat and stared at Judy, not saying a word. She turned to her father and, raising her face, kissed him tenderly on the cheek.

"Well, good night, Daddy," she said. She walked across the room, her skirts swaying and her soft hair moving gently across the collar of her cape. Bending down, she kissed her mother lightly. "Good night," she said again.

"Have a nice time, darling."

Judy shrugged her shoulders and smiled. Her eyes drooped wearily. "Well, you know parties," she said. She nodded brightly to Lois and swept from the room, followed by Haskell Cummings, who had managed to mutter something that sounded like "Good night."

Judy stood to one side, waiting for Haskell to open the front door for her. "I do love to dance, though," she said. "Don't you?" She went out and Haskell followed her, closing the door behind him.

Mr. and Mrs. Graves looked at one another. "She had lipstick on," Lois said. "And powder. And nail polish. And that Haskell Cummings acted like a dope."

Mr. Graves jingled the coins in his pocket. "Can you beat it!" he said. "She sold him down the river. Sold him down the river, by God!" His voice was rich with pride and satisfaction. "By God, if she didn't!"